VOLUME 8
story **Yuyuko Takemiya**
illustrations **Yasu**

Everyone, it's almost time for the school trip!

Aren't you looking forward to it?!

Do you have any places you really want to go?

Takasu Ryuuji
"Maybe hell...or purgatory...
Well, we're going to Okinawa, though.
Okinawa...ahh..."

You don't seem too excited. Did
something happen over winter break?

"I was hospitalized with the
flu for a while..."

Kitamura Yuusaku

"What's with the glum face?! The school trip is part of our studies!

We're going to Okinawa! The hotel is in Naha! Plus, this is the first time I'll ever be on a plane!

Like it or not, our expectations are sky-high! We'll roar over the southern sea, that's how I lead!"

Hey, that's our Kitamura-kun! Wouldn't expect less from the student council president and class rep! But, other than Okinawa, is there anywhere else you want to go?

"Why are you asking that? Okinawa is undoubtedly the best choice there is! Blow, winds of the Ryukyu Kingdom!"

Kushieda Minori
"First meditation, pineapple! Chomp chomp chomp!
Delicious—it's delicious~! It's so sweet and juicy!

Second meditation, Okinawa Soba!
Slurp slurp slurp! Delicious—it's delicious~!
They piled on the pork rib!

Third meditation, Blue Seal Ice Cream!
Lick lick lick! It's delicious!"

Stop this gourmet delusion! It's scary!
Actually, a-are you really looking forward to Okinawa that much?
It's the middle of winter, and it's not the best season to go…

"Ha, that's absurd—my body is armed with muscles
of steel. There's no difference between the middle
of winter or the middle of summer to me!"

Kawashima Ami

"Wouldn't it be so great to go shopping in New York or Paris? A full tour of Europe wouldn't be bad, either. I'd really like to go to Vienna or Switzerland, and I'd really like to go to Italy, too. Oh, but what if someone tried to scout me? I don't know what I'd do. No way! I only speak Japanese! ♥"

Well…um…we're just a normal high school and can't really do that.

"I know that. I just said it because you asked. Well, Okinawa's pretty great. It's too cold to get in the ocean, but we can swim in the pools at least, right~?"

Toradora! 8

BY

Yuyuko Takemiya

ILLUSTRATED BY

Yasu

Seven Seas Entertainment

TORADORA! Vol. 8

© YUYUKO TAKEMIYA 2008

First published in Japan in 2008 by KADOKAWA
CORPORATION, Tokyo. English translation rights arranged
with KADOKAWA CORPORATION, Tokyo.

Seven Seas press and purchase enquiries can be sent to
Marketing Manager Lianne Sentar at press@gomanga.com.
Information regarding the distribution and purchase of
digital editions is available from Digital Manager CK Russell
at digital@gomanga.com.

Seven Seas and the Seven Seas logo are trademarks of
Seven Seas Entertainment. All rights reserved.

Follow Seven Seas Entertainment online at
sevenseasentertainment.com.

TRANSLATION: Jan Cash & Vincent Castaneda
ADAPTATION: Will Holcomb
COVER DESIGN: Nicky Lim
INTERIOR LAYOUT & DESIGN: Clay Gardner
PROOFREADER: Jade Gardner, Rebecca Schneidereit
LIGHT NOVEL EDITOR: Nibedita Sen
MANAGING EDITOR: Julie Davis
EDITOR-IN-CHIEF: Adam Arnold
PUBLISHER: Jason DeAngelis

ISBN: 978-1-64275-739-2
Printed in USA
First Printing: December 2019
10 9 8 7 6 5 4 3 2

ToC
Table of Contents

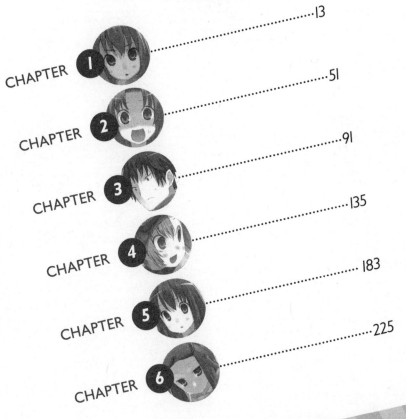

IT WAS TWELVE PAST ELEVEN in the evening.

In forty-eight more minutes, the day would end.

As his breath fogged white, Takasu Ryuuji looked up at the night sky through his still-open window. That night, the moon and the stars were hidden behind the inky clouds. His already gloomy mood darkened.

That night was particularly cold. The below-freezing wind pricked at his skin. His body, clothed only in a parka and tracksuit bottoms, trembled slightly, and he felt like his teeth had been chattering forever. His dry lips were stiff, his toes were numb, and his heart—well, it had frozen over long ago.

Ever since that night on Christmas Eve.

Since that night, Ryuuji had been wandering in the darkness of absolute zero.

"I hope...tomorrow never comes..."

With the lights still off in the room, he sat clumsily on the window frame. The sliding frame of the window steadied his back as he breathed a long sigh. He pushed up his now grown-out bangs and hugged one of his knees to himself. He pulled his parka over his cold and smarting ears to protect them from the wind and then narrowed his eyes. He held his breath, mostly unconsciously, and gritted his chattering teeth.

The new year had come and gone a week ago.

Tomorrow, they would start a new semester at school.

Once they started a new semester, then he basically couldn't avoid seeing *her*. Whenever he thought about that, whenever he imagined it, Ryuuji's heart seemed to grate to the point it seemed close to breaking. No matter how deeply he breathed in, there wasn't enough air. He was suffocating. Every morning, every day, every night, without warning, his mind would revive *her* form and voice. His brain would vividly and mercilessly replay out his thoughts from spring, summer, fall, and the events of that night.

"What expression am I even supposed to have when I see her...?" he groaned in a low voice. His empty eyes wandered through the air. Even in his thoughts, he couldn't meet her eyes. He didn't know how he could see her face-to-face when she was real.

He held his head and bit his peeling lips. The taste of blood spread lightly over his tongue. His pupils were as wide as they could go, and he had bags under his eyes that were dark enough to look like someone had jokingly drawn them on his face. Ryuuji hadn't been able to sleep for days now, and it had reduced his face to that of someone just waiting for their arrest. It was easy to visualize. One day, out of nowhere, the police would make their way up into his house, coming in without even taking off their shoes. They would have been tipped off by the neighbors. His hands would be restrained behind him. The police would be yelling.

"The kitchen looks fishy!"

"Oh! I found something! We got some white powder in here!"

...No, that's just potato starch!

"Ha ha ha...ha ha...ha..."

Idiotic.

As he laughed emptily, his thoughts drifted far away. *Even if it's because of a misunderstanding, if I were to get arrested, at least I wouldn't have to go to school.* He was half-serious.

He pushed at the dirt caught in the window's frame with unconscious fingertips. It happened a little after that.

"Uh..."

The window of the condo across from him lit up with blinding light. The inside of the room, which was left bare by the drawn-back curtains, was easy to see into. He also saw the shadow of a petite person cut across the room.

That person, of course, was the owner of the place next door that had been silent until now. It was Aisaka Taiga, with her unmistakable long, fluffy hair and her pale white face. In light blue pajamas with a white cardigan layered on top, Taiga walked through her bedroom, which was about as large as the Takasus' whole apartment. Then, she seemed to notice Ryuuji's eyes on her and turned to face him.

"Yo...Taiga."

He got up a bit and lightly raised a hand to her—just as she exclaimed, "Wha?! What are you doing?!"

Ugh!

This is the worst.

Why'd I have to get spotted by someone so annoying?

Or so Taiga's face very clearly said. *Okay, I'll just ignore him. Pretend I never saw him.* Her expression was so obvious, he could even glean that much. Their eyes had clearly met, but she flipped her hair around, turned her back to him, and hid herself in a corner of the room Ryuuji couldn't see. She even harshly pulled the curtains closed.

Had he done something wrong? Feeling the empathy of an honest person, Ryuuji reflexively put his hand to his chest and tried to think over his own actions until that day, but he couldn't come up with a single reason why Taiga would be coldly ignoring him.

"What is it with you...? Why are you suddenly ignoring me...? Taiga! I saw all of that! Why are you ignoring me?!" he shouted without thinking.

He'd completely forgotten about the neighbors. This was just too much, after all. Taiga knew his circumstances. She was being this cold to him when he was in a spiritual crisis. And it wasn't just this time, either. He hadn't been able to get a grasp on her attitude for the last few days.

"Hey! Open that up a little! There was something I've been wanting to tell you!"

No response. She must have heard him, though.

"Taiga! Damn it... Is this the silent treatment? I can't believe you'd do that to me! Just watch!"

Silent curses overflowed from every pore in Ryuuji's body. He oozed with dark feelings as he glared over at the window. The negative emotions that had gathered awakened his evil face. *I'll wipe this planet from the Milky Way!* it seemed to say.

With his face like that, he made his way to the entrance and back, bringing the deck brush with him. He braced his legs around the window and, hanging onto the sash, leaned out with the brush in his free hand.

"Taiga! Taiga! Hey, let me see your face! I know you heard me! Taiga!"

Bang bang bang bang bang thud bang bang thud bang bang bang bang bang! BANG! He banged the long brush's wooden handle against Taiga's bedroom window in succession. He was hitting it almost hard enough to break it.

Normally, he wasn't allowed to do this. It would have damaged the glass, and he had once hit Taiga hard in the face doing this in the past. But, this night, he would use his last resort.

Vibrations stronger than any alarm clock rang out through the silent night.

"Hey, what do you think you're doing?!"

Of course, even Taiga couldn't ignore that. She threw open the curtains completely with a terrific force, and their faces met for the first time in a while.

"Eek!" Ryuuji was taken aback. Her face, which was made up beautifully like a French doll's, was contorted terribly.

"Don't..." Her unpleasant mood now fully exposed by the fully open window, Taiga grabbed the end of the deck brush that was pointed at her. Then, with ridiculous strength, she pulled it toward herself.

"...get carried..."

"Ah, wha, whoa?!"

Ryuuji lost his balance. He reeled forward and started to fall face-first towards the ground several meters below.

"Naaaaaaaaaah!"

—Or at least, he had just been about to.

Stars blinked in front of his eyes. "Gah!" By the time he realized it was his own voice that had shouted, he was already falling backwards onto his bed. He had been whacked right in the face with the deck brush just as he began to fall forward.

"Keh! You pig!"

Slam! The windows closed, and he heard the noise of the curtain prickling his skull.

Then he was left alone in the silence.

"Te..."

Terrible. That was just too horrible.

"T-t-te..."

His eyes, which had been scrubbed by the brush, reflexively started to overflow with tears, and snot ran down to his mouth.

"Te...te-te..."

Still on the bed, he held his face, with no idea anymore if he was crying or smiling. The voice in which Taiga had spat "Keh! You pig!" at him still distinctly stabbed at his ears. *A pig,* he thought. *So I'm a pig.* With his own swinish nature thrust into his face, he arduously made his way back up and clung to the window. He latched on to the curtains.

"Terrrr-te-te-te...!"

He glared at the window across from him. That was the Palmtop Tiger for you. She would resort to brutal means and do so spectacularly. After wounding his soul with one bite, she had completely shattered it. Even though he couldn't form his admiration into words, he kept trying to convey his feelings to her.

"Could you shut up?! What do you think—"

"Eiiiie, te-te-te!"

"Gyaaaaaaaah!"

Taiga opened the window again out of irritation and then yelled as she saw Ryuuji laughing and crying. She fell back onto her butt—Ryuuji saw her feet fly into the air. *Eeek?!* Without thinking, he thrust out a hand that wouldn't reach her.

"A-all you are is an actual troublemaker! When you tempt the gods, you invite cruel outcomes like these... How frightening! Ryuuji, your face goes beyond human reason!" Finally getting back up, Taiga spoke as his outstretched arm scratched at empty air.

"Th-that's the first time in my life that someone has said anything as terrible as that to me!" said Ryuuji. "No, actually, more importantly, how could you scratch my face with a deck brush?! Do you know where that brush goes?! I retired it from washing the bath to washing the entrance and the outside passage and the outside stairs! The drain got super clogged with garbage, and I scrubbed it like this first when it was dry and then scraped it when it was wet—"

"Enough with the chitchat. It's time to sleep, you freak! Tch, you're too loud... You've got a face like a dog that would come at you in *Resident Evil*..."

"What did you call me?! If you hadn't been ignoring me in the first place, we wouldn't have gotten in this mess! Oh, and right... How...how dare you ignore me! You know that I'm heartbroken right now, too! I-I can't believe that you-you would—"

"Like I care!"

"What?!"

After giving him that shockingly direct reply, Taiga haughtily stuck out her chin and looked down upon Ryuuji's face with arrogance. She snorted, her large eyes as emotionless as if they were looking at dog crap by the roadside.

"I've got things to do. I can't always be entertaining you."

"Wh-what did you just say?! There's no way you could have anything to do. You're always bored to tears!"

"You can say whatever you want. You don't have to understand. There's no way someone with such a small and poor measuring stick as you could measure the ideals behind the actions of someone as large and as rich as me."

"Who's going on about being large and rich when you've got a grain of rice for a face?!"

The moment he returned her poison, he heard a sound.

Ring ring ring. Ring ring ring ring.

"Oh. Time's up."

The idiotic Caramell melody came from the cell phone Taiga was holding. At that weak tone, Ryuuji's strength also disappeared. He didn't know what it was time for, but...

"Well, that's how it is. The new semester starts tomorrow, so why don't you go to bed soon? Rather than complaining at me, you can think over the mountain of things I'm sure you need to do."

How cold. The chilliness permeated through him. He looked back at Taiga's face in spite of himself as she quickly tried to close the window and cloister herself in.

"So that's how it is..."

"What?"

At the words Ryuuji let slip out, Taiga's cute face formed a heartfelt scowl. How could she act like another human being was such a chore?

"So you actually couldn't care less about it, then..."

Taiga had cried, at first, when he told her what happened on Christmas Eve. Ryuuji bit his lip as he looked at her in shock. Were the tears from that day fake?

"You're not lying, right?"

"I can't believe Minori would reject you—you're kidding."

It had happened while he had been hospitalized for the flu at the end of the year. It had been three days since the party. Once Ryuuji regained the use of his mouth, he had completely opened up to Taiga about what happened on the night of Christmas Eve. He told her what happened after she sent him off.

Taiga, whom Yasuko had sent to him with a change of clothes, started to cry after she heard that. She sobbed to the point she couldn't even hide it under the large mask she had been required to put on.

"Why did this happen? That can't be true."

Taiga had covered her eyes with her little hands and, still sitting by his bedside, cried for a while. Lying there, Ryuuji couldn't stand it, and his sanpaku eyes had pitifully teared up, too.

Regardless, Ryuuji had felt just a little bit better at Taiga's tears. He was thankful for the miracle of having someone by his side who received sadness with sadness and who cried together with him when he was hurt. He just couldn't believe he had someone who understood that he had been hurt and who would be sad with him. He still couldn't believe it.

But where did that all go?

"Could you stop venting at me because Minorin rejected you?"

Deep wrinkles appeared on Taiga's forehead. She stuck her finger into her ear and fished around with it.

"I said I've got something I need to do. Ahhh, look...because you've been meaninglessly chattering away, it's probably gotten all soggy."

As she said that, she brought *it* over to the window from where she had placed it on a desk nearby. She heartily pried off the top.

"I-Is that what you needed to do?!" Ryuuji said.

He was so taken aback, he couldn't say anything more. The reason Taiga had so gloomily ignored him was...

"Tch, you're such a loudmouth. I'll eat it here, okay. Hmph, I'm digging in."

Sl-slurpppppppp! It was cup ramen.

"You...you...you really are..."

"Mm, delicious! What?"

She looked like she was in heaven as she ate a mouthful of noodles, slurping them up energetically. At Taiga's carefree face, Ryuuji's heart splintered and ran to waste.

"I don't care anymore. It's nothing."

He clammed up.

"I see."

Sl-sl-sl-sluuuuuurp!

"I hope you bloat up. I hope your face puffs up in a hurry for the new semester."

Dark Ryuuji had emerged. His raised sanpaku eyes flickered repulsively with murky fire.

However, Taiga just half-laughed, "Heh. Fine by me. I already know what I'm getting into by eating ramen at this time of night."

She cradled her ramen as she arrogantly stuck out her flat chest. On her white cardigan were droplets from her spoon that formed the shape of the big dipper. She hadn't noticed.

Ahh. What kind of fate had led the rental and condo to be next to each other? Ryuuji and Taiga's rooms faced one another, just two meters apart. They were both on the second floor, with eye-to-eye south-facing and north-facing windows.

Ryuuji stood speechless next to the window in his bedroom and simply watched Taiga's cheeks as she happily slurped her ramen. He looked like he wanted to fill her mouth with firecrackers—but not really. He'd lost sight of the earlier melancholy that had filled his mind. His mental landscape was currently that of a wandering ghost ship, roaming the sea of spirits. They were incompetent at navigation, the passengers had been annihilated, and the captain was a skeleton.

"Is that all you're eating for dinner?" the ghostly crew member, Ryuuji, asked her in a low voice from the ship's deck.

"Nooo. Around nine I ate a meat bun, mayo corn bread, and an éclair. This is a midnight snack."

"That's the worst menu ever. You had to have gotten it all from the convenience store."

Taiga still had her chopsticks in her mouth as she turned away, playing dumb. She said neither yes nor no, so Ryuuji had probably been on the mark.

"What is it with you... Seriously."

Creak, creak, creak. The ghost ship screeched on the haunted sea, pulled into a dark whirlpool of grudges and curses that even the rudder couldn't break through.

"You don't come over... You stuff yourself with that stuff...and don't even eat your vegetables..."

"What about it? Oh, you must have wanted to have ramen, too. Wow, how greedy you are."

"I don't want any! You're seriously getting on my nerves! You really are... You just push my buttons!"

As he groaned, Ryuuji scratched at his head. He writhed and howled at the night sky. His already dangerous-looking yakuza face started to transform perilously into something he couldn't reveal to others. It was sharp, treacherous, and vulgar.

"I've been wanting to ask you this for a while! Why won't you come over?! Plus, why have you been ignoring me like you just did earlier?! What's going on with you?!"

Dark curses came steaming from each and every one of the pores on his body, and he knew it. In the opposite window, Taiga scrunched up her face as though she had seen something unpleasant. *Mood killer.* He knew that she was mouthing those words with her rosy lips, but he was ticked off and couldn't help it.

"What is it with *you?*" she asked. "I told you not to take things out on other people."

"I'm not taking anything out on you! I'm actually mad at *you!*"

He was going against the most dangerous living being in the world, the Palmtop Tiger. Ryuuji brandished his murder weapon of a face as he spat at her.

"I-Is it because I'm too annoying for you now that I've been hurt?! Is that it?! Is it because I'm too depressing for you to talk to?! Am I wrong to think that?! Am I just a nuisance now that I'm a mess?! Am I just in the way?! You were sympathizing with me to start with! What was that?! What was it?! It's not like I asked you to keep moping around with me! I didn't ask you to console me! But you could at least be as close as you were before, like normal!"

"Huh?"

"Don't say 'Huh!'"

He knew.

Taiga was obviously trying to distance herself from him. *Why are you doing this?!* he wanted to shout.

When he was hospitalized, she would help out, since Yasuko couldn't not go to work. She would bring him clothes, go shopping, and gallantly help with all kinds of things for Ryuuji's care. But once Ryuuji was discharged, Taiga flat out wouldn't come over to the Takasus'.

She would make up whatever excuse she could and refuse breakfast, lunch, and dinner. Even on days when she shouldn't have been busy, she would leave her condo without so much as showing her face to them. When he finally did see her, like now, she was happily eating cup ramen. If she'd only come over to the Takasus', there was plenty of food, and he had told her to come and eat. Even when she said she didn't need it, he made enough for Taiga every day. He would save the food for her. Yasuko was waiting, too.

"I wonder what's gotten into Taiga-chan lately. She won't come even when you invite her?"

Even Yasuko was a little down.

They'd even put out the sitting cushion Taiga monopolized where she normally sat.

"That's right—you just think I'm gloomy after being rejected by Kushieda! Ah, that must be right. I'm depressing! I'm so sorry about that!"

His voice went hoarse as he shouted, and his face looked like that of a demon crawling from hell. He knew that he was being disgraceful and uncool, but feelings brewing in his stomach wouldn't stop now that he'd found a path to release them. He flung his arms around and kept howling.

"Ahgh, I don't care anymore! I just don't care! In the end, you're abandoning me for being such a letdown! That's right! Ahh, you could've just said so! You just want to throw your relationship with me away like trash! I'm just a nuisance, and you don't need me at all! I get it, I get it all. It's fine, I'd just rather you tell it to me directly, I'd rather hear it from your mouth...oh!"

"Shut up, you foolish bug."

She was a second faster than he could finish. She threw one of her chopsticks like a dart, aiming right for the middle of Ryuuji's forehead. It didn't pierce him, but the force with which it hit hurt quite a bit, and Ryuuji was left speechless despite himself.

"You really are a stupid bug. Don't you go getting deranged on me, you insolent pest."

Taiga tried to snap the other chopstick in half but broke a third of it off instead. She clumsily used the pieces to chug the rest of her ramen, her large eyes fixed on Ryuuji. She had gone beyond scorn and had become pitying.

"Do I need to explain it to you from the start?" she said.

"Explain what?"

"I'm doing all this because of you. The heavens must be in an uproar right around now. They're so shocked that someone like me, more merciful than the gods or Buddha, has appeared. In the past, I was like, 'Ryuuji's an idiot, an idiot, an idiot, an idiot, a suuuuper big idiot,' but—"

"Did you really think that little of me?"

"—but seeing you sink this low is really just shocking. You must be the king of idiots."

"You avoid me, don't come over to eat, don't show your face, and ignore me... Are you saying that's all supposed to be for my sake?"

"That's right. But actually, it's for you and for Minorin's sake." Taiga inhaled and looked at Ryuuji for a moment. "Listen. You know, I thought about it while you were hospitalized and I was watching you sleep."

She dipped her head like a drooping flower bud, brought one hand up to her own chest, and shook her head with sorrow. "Ahh, your face was so terrifying, I just couldn't help but want to do something—bwa ha ha!"

Unable to keep a straight face any longer, she began to splutter. Ryuuji slammed his window closed. *No way! That was a joke just now! Open up!* He could hear Taiga wailing in a way that would bother the neighbors.

Given no other choice, he opened the window again to yell at her. "I've really got my back up against the wall when it comes to my mental state! If you joke around this time, I'll really, definitely, just drop dead!"

"Okay, okay. I got it. I'll be serious. Right...serious. After all that happened, I was thinking. And that's when I understood it. I understood completely from the bottom of my heart, like an idiot."

"Are you referring to me?"

"No. I mean me."

Taiga twisted her lips as though mocking herself and shrugged. She closed her eyes to declare that the joke was over and she was being serious.

"I thought, what was I even doing? Like, I was being such an idiot, wasn't I?"

The shadows of the night reflected darkly in the eyes she slowly opened. She tangled her fingers in her hair and combed it out. She put her elbows on the windowsill and looked up at the starless sky. The line of her chin seemed to glow white even in the dark.

Her quiet voice slid slowly into the stillness of the night.

"I said I'd support you and Minorin being together, but I was always hanging around your place. Of course Minorin took that the wrong way. Even if I told her not to, it's not like she couldn't think that was what was going on. That's normal, isn't it? I can't believe we... Well, I can't believe I didn't think about it. I was just clinging to you. I really am an idiot."

Taiga smoothed her bangs, which had been ruffled by the freezing wind, and then smiled faintly at him. Their eyes met directly, and Ryuuji felt just very slightly at a loss.

"In other words, you—" He averted his eyes as he put his next words together. The cold wind stung his skin. "—you think that the reason Kushieda rejected me was because she still misunderstood our relationship?"

From the corner of his eye, he saw Taiga nod.

"So, our co-living situation is now over. I'm starting up on my own. I'm not just saying it this time. I'll really try to do it."

"...Kushieda might misunderstand, so you won't come over anymore?"

"Yeah. I'm not coming over anymore."

Silence fell over the two of them. The icy night seemed to have frozen over into an unendingly dark and motionless state. Though he was silent, Ryuuji didn't agree with Taiga. Instead, he licked his dry lips.

"You stopped coming over, and... So you're saying this because you actually want me and Kushieda to be together? You don't think that Kushieda just doesn't like me?"

"I don't." Taiga's answer, however, was filled with conviction. "I think that Minorin does like you. I can tell just by looking, but she's just hung up on me. That's the only reason I can think of.

Why do *you* think that Minorin rejected you? Do you actually think she doesn't like you?"

"I..."

Ryuuji was touched. He held his breath for a moment and scratched at his head. He didn't know whether it was okay to say this, even as he squeezed out the words.

"I don't know if that's right or not. When I say I don't know... I mean that I really can't avoid thinking that Kushieda might not have liked me at all. I just can't accept that she rejected me to the point she didn't even let me confess to her, actually."

He closed his eyes and thought of her—of Kushieda Minori.

"In other words, I thought like she did have slight feelings for me, too. But it might be shameless and self-centered for me to think that..."

"Taaakaaasuuu-kun! Hey, yo, my man!"

The Minori in his mind smiled brightly. She breakdanced in the air. Her eyes, which contained something unknown to Ryuuji, looked straight at him. Sometimes they wavered, sometimes they saw right through him, sometimes they were hard. Those eyes had captured Ryuuji and wouldn't let him go.

"But then she rejected me so easily. Well, she didn't so much reject me...as just not even let me tell her I liked her. I'm such a mess... I can't just give up. I think."

He knew that her fingertips were as hot as fire. Even now, he couldn't forget that heat or the time she asked him to buy the Lucky Man race picture where they were holding hands. He could never forget the tone of her voice. He couldn't forget the soft vibration hiding behind the faint tremor in her words.

Through their normal, everyday conversations, hadn't Minori tried to slowly shed light on the secrets of her heart?

Ryuuji couldn't forget her eyes, her voice, her expression. There had to have been something more to it than what he could see. She must have had some feelings for him. There must have been a small chance that she did...

He was pitiful, and he knew it, but he still couldn't abandon the idea. He held his head and groaned.

"I-I-I...I don't know. I have no idea. Maybe it was my imagination? Maybe it was all a convenient delusion? But I can't...believe that. No matter what, I can't think that's how it is."

"Me neither..." Taiga whispered in a low voice. "I don't think it was your imagination, either."

Ryuuji opened his eyes slightly. Taiga was still looking straight at him. Her eyes let off a strong light. They didn't falter or waver, and her gaze stayed trained on him.

"Don't run away." Her voice echoed around them. "You still like Minorin, don't you? You believe that Minorin has feelings for you, don't you? Then you can't run away. You need to keep thinking of Minorin, and once she sees that I'm not hanging around and living with you, she'll definitely give you a different answer. That's what I think. So you can't get all gloomy and worried like that. You can't say you're just fine with this, either."

"But—"

"No buts. I'm actually really sort of afraid of seeing Minorin, too." As though trying to fake out of the end of her sentence, Taiga snorted.

"Why?"

"You don't get it? Who was the one who got Minori to go to the place where she rejected you?"

Oh. Ryuuji remembered the details of that night he had wanted to forget. *Right.* The angel Taiga had convinced Minori to come to the party and, at the party, she had rejected him in one fell swoop.

"And this is what ended up happening... Since then, I haven't even seen Minorin. Minorin had softball this whole time, and after that, she went to stay at her grandmother's house with the rest of her family for the end of the year. I haven't heard Minorin's side of what happened on Christmas Eve. I was insistent about her going to you. She can't pretend it didn't happen."

At that point, Taiga bit her bottom lip slightly. She rubbed roughly at her forehead as her white breath puffed out. "Ugh." Her whisper seemed aimed at herself, and it was filled with regret she couldn't hide.

"If I hadn't forced Minorin out because I was so excited about Christmas, this wouldn't have happened. Don't you think that?"

"Like I would."

His low reply was how he really felt. He had been afraid of what would happen, but the one who wanted to confess, who decided to, and who ran back to school during the night was all Ryuuji.

But Taiga continued. "It's what I think."

Sorry, she was saying. It wasn't like her.

After having that done to him, and being apologized to, and her trying to take the blame on herself, he didn't know whether his heart could beat harder. His already-damaged pride had been smashed even further into pieces, but Taiga didn't know that. If she'd been sitting in a corner of that dark, small room with him, he would have hit the top of her head really hard and said, "You don't understand the subtleties of the heart!"

But right now, he couldn't even do that.

"But! I won't run away! So—" Taiga's finger suddenly pointed straight at Ryuuji's heart. "*You* can't run away. You can't run from this situation. I know it's hard, but...if you run away, then it's really over."

He felt like his heart had stopped. *Then it's really over...* He held his breath for a moment at the impact of those words.

"Answer me, Ryuu-flea."

"Who's Ryuu-flea...?"

"Have you prepared yourself to not run away?"

Ryuuji somehow nodded. Seeing that, Taiga seemed to prepare herself for something; the edges of her mouth pulled back faintly.

"From here on, you don't need to wake me up in the morning. I don't need a bento or dinner. I'll figure things out myself somehow. I'll do all the housework by myself, too. Minorin thinks that I need you. That's why I want to prove to her that I can make it alone. I want to show that to Minorin. And then, we wait for Minorin to give you a different answer."

She said it simply and abruptly, and then slapped her own cheeks. It seemed she really meant it. Without realizing it, Ryuuji blinked, as though he had seen something blinding while he looked at Taiga.

Taiga, apparently, really was tougher than he was.

He wanted to kick himself for complaining. He wanted to slap himself for thinking that he would be lonely. Feeling himself cheering up, Ryuuji nodded for her.

He didn't really think that things with Minori would go well if he and Taiga spent time apart. It wasn't that simple, but that also wasn't the important part. Now that Taiga was finally acting more like an adult and trying to stand on her own, he didn't want to show his pitiful face to her. He didn't want to be overtaken by Taiga as she grew up, or be left behind.

He didn't want to be a wimp who had been rejected. He didn't want to stagnate while dilly-dallying around.

He didn't want his long-unrequited love to end like that.

"I got it. I'll do what I can. But...please just don't burn the place down."

Taiga thrust out her chest, filled with as much confidence as the continental shelf. "Yeah, it'll be fine. I swear I won't use the stove. I swear I'll eat takeout forever!"

She had said something that was so low level, it was embarrassing. Ryuuji sighed despite himself.

"I wonder how long that can last..."

"What?! It'll work! For eternity and beyond!"

He looked at Taiga, who was breathing roughly. Even though her cheeks and nose were red from the cold wind, there was a fearless smile on her face, and she seemed absurd in her pride.

"I'll be fine now, so anyway, you do what you need to. Okay? First you need to find out Minorin's true feelings. I've already prepared an opportunity for that."

"An opportunity?"

"Yeah. It was a lucky strike of fate." Taiga nodded and then coolly closed her window. "Good night."

Or at least, she tried to do it coolly. She got four fingers caught in the window, and her shriek echoed loudly in the silent night.

He wouldn't run.

And then, he would find out how she really felt.

He was prepared, but it was far from morning and the world was dark, so he couldn't even see what he wanted. He didn't know what the opportunity Taiga spoke of was, either.

Ryuuji still couldn't fall asleep, so he wrapped himself in the heavy blanket and stared vacantly at the ceiling. Once morning came, it would be a new semester. He didn't have any say in that. They would see each other again at school.

If only morning would never come. Did thinking that also count as running?

"Mooorrrrrnnniiiiinnngggggg!"

Ryuuji trembled slightly.

"Inko-chan, how excited you are right in the morning..."

Normally, the Takasus' house was dim in the mornings. And cold. Even though they were indoors, their breath would be white, and the hands they used to refill Inko-chan's water and food would be numb.

Despite the gloomy winter morning, Inko-chan was happy about something. She spread her scaly, plucked wings inside her cage and yelled. "Mooorrrnnniiiiinnggg! Moooorrrrrnn-niiiiinnggggg!"

The cloudy whites of her eyes had a green tint to them, covered by the mesh-like pattern of blood vessels. Her mulberry-colored beak gaped open unreservedly.

"Morning! Morning! Morning! Morning!"

"Oh, wait! Inko-chan, hey, stop! Stop that! Ah!"

The parakeet slipped past Ryuuji's hand and escaped from the cage. Inko-chan went at a speed that might have been fast enough to break the sound barrier. *Do do do do do do do!* She slipped past him, kicking bamboo splinters from the tatami, and ran as fast as she could. She was like a frilled lizard sprinting across a desert. As if trying to make a fool of her owner, who was chasing after her on his knees, she juked to the right and left.

Why is this happening first thing in the morning? Ryuuji's wrinkles might have been as deep as the Fossa Magna. At that point, a light bulb suddenly switched on in his mind. That speed.

The suddenness of her turns. That artistic footwork. He felt he had seen it somewhere before.

"Zidane! This is Zidane's Marseille Roulette!"

Ryuuji's sanpaku eyes opened wide, and he covered his mouth. He'd never imagined that the ugly parakeet he was raising was a member of the Galacticos.

"Just kidding...ha ha."

Unable to keep going with the joke he himself had started, Ryuuji simply sat down. He really wished morning hadn't come. He had prayed and prayed and prayed, but in the end, here it was.

On the other hand, Inko-chan, aka Takasu Zidane, was in a state of excitement whose cause was unknown. She circled her owner, who was emitting a dark aura, with amazing speed. She switched tracks and slipped right through the cracked sliding door into Yasuko's room. *Shooooom!*

Ryuuji heard various shrieks that he wouldn't have thought had come from a person. "Hngaaat? Ungggha!" He also heard the sound of a scuffle on top of the futon bed.

"Faaaaaaaaaaah! Now I'm aaaawwwwwaaaaakkkkkeee!"

There it was. Someone wearing a tracksuit soaked head to toe with the smell of alcohol, and her curly hair poofed out like an afro, crawled from the bedroom's open door. Ryuuji scowled in surprise.

"A country bumpkin..."

"Fueh?"

Grasped in the hand of his mother, who had come home drunk that morning, was Ryuuji's Zidane. Inko-chan flopped over.

"Ahh wah! If you hold her that hard, she'll die!"

"Buuuuuuuuut! Inko-chan was running on my face!"

Then, still grasped in her hand, Zidane...

"Blergh..."

...threw up.

Whoa! Nagh! The mother and son's shrieks echoed through the room. After making a commotion right from the morning Zidane must have suffered the natural consequences of her own actions. Like a geyser, Inko-chan spurted green mucus-like liquid onto Yasuko's chin.

"Wah! ★! Uwahah! Uwahahahah. I'm done for! Blergh! ★"

Yasuko threw the parakeet at her son and stumbled away without looking back. She headed straight to the toilet. A sound Ryuuji couldn't stand echoed through the apartment, and he couldn't block his ears no matter how he tried. In his right hand was the Zidane that had been thrust at him—no. It was now just a parakeet covered in puke.

He sighed. Ryuuji gently wiped Inko-chan down with a damp tissue, but there was a stain he couldn't get out no matter how much he rubbed. When he looked really, really closely, Inko-chan's feathers made a pattern that looked exactly like the face of a dying person.

He gently put Inko-chan back in her cage and had her grip her perch. Ryuuji whispered in a low voice as his eyes flashed blue like a lustrous Japanese sword. "Are you okay after throwing up, Inko-chan? Should we go to the vet? We just have the opening ceremony today, anyway. I could take off from school and take you there..."

Don't run away. The sound of Taiga's voice from the night before sincerely echoed in his mind, but this wasn't the same as running. Inko-chan wasn't doing well and he was seriously concerned, so he had to do it.

However, his attempts at excuses were futile.

"Morning...morning...it's morning!"

As though trying to regain her lost calories, Inko-chan was aggressively starting to go after the fresh COLZA clothes pinned to her cage. She'd already forgotten Ryuuji. Inko-chan was so perfectly healthy that there was no point in even saying it out loud.

Inko-chan, it couldn't be that you—

"You weren't making a big deal in order to cheer me up...were you?"

Well, it didn't matter. It didn't. No, really.

Ryuuji turned his eyes away with all his strength from the idiotic face of the idiotic bird. He breathed in and stood up. He washed his hands and then washed the cup that Yasuko seemed to have used when she got home in the morning. He quickly wiped away the water on the sink with a dishtowel and confirmed with himself that he really didn't feel like making breakfast. Then, when he looked at the clock, he realized the incident had taken up a lot more time than he could afford to waste.

"Ahhh... I don't want to go..."

Don't run away.

Okay, okay, I got it. I'll go. He wasn't brave enough to skip out on the school's opening ceremony in the first place, anyway.

He pulled his neatly hung school jacket off its dry-cleaning hanger and, mostly out of unconscious habit, brushed it. He put a loose-knit sweater over his shirt. It was a thick gray V-neck cardigan. After that, he put on his school jacket. He didn't hook it at the top but just buttoned it. Then he wrapped himself in his cashmere scarf, which Taiga had used indiscriminately, and was done with his preparations. Though it was the middle of winter, Ryuuji didn't wear a coat on principle. He didn't want to end up looking like a student in the middle of exams.

He'd packed his tote bag the night before, and he had his cell phone and keys. With that, all he had to do was leave the house.

"I really don't want to go..."

No, he would go. *I'll go, I will, I really will.* He shook his head twice, three times, and somehow shook off the gloominess building up in it.

He dully called out to Yasuko, who was washing her mouth at the sink. "I'm going..."

"See you 'ater...ack, wight, Ryuu-chaaan."

Even after throwing up so much, Yasuko was still drunk and spoke with a shaky command of Japanese as she raised her head.

"I didn' forget~! I remembered! ★ I signed it and left it on the table in the room!"

"What was it again?"

"Huh~? Really, Ryuu-chan, you can't be all forgetful like you have been lately! It's the Okinawa thing~!"

Okinawa?

Okinawa!

He was bathed in the smell of thick alcohol breath that came straight at his face. *Right*. He remembered. Flustered, Ryuuji went back in to get it.

"That was close. I almost completely forgot."

What had been left in Yasuko's room was the permission slip for the school trip they would go on that month. It was a form for getting permission from a parent or guardian for the deposit and insurance. With everything that had happened recently, it had completely left his mind that he had been told to bring it to the opening ceremony. Yasuko's excuse for a brain had remembered, but he hadn't... How pitiful.

"Okinawa, Okinawa! That sounds nice, it's luxurious~! I wish I could go, too!"

"Well, I'm headed out..."

"Ohhh...looks like you're down?"

Ryuuji thrust the printout into his bag, put on his perfectly polished shoes, and then simply opened the front door. Just as he did, the midwinter northerly wind blew in, and he accidentally closed his eyes at the chill.

Ryuu-chaan, are you okay? He could hear Yasuko's carefree voice coming from inside the room, but he already didn't have the energy to answer her. It was super cold, but the morning light was strangely bright, and his sharp eyes shone as if they would be more at home in the dead of night at Kabukicho—Shinjuku's red light district.

This isn't the time for me to be thinking about Okinawa. His heels clunked as he went down the iron stairs.

The asphalt reflected the morning sun to an unnecessary degree. He looked at the entrance of Taiga's condo from the corner of his eye. The polished white marble stairs made a perfect arch as they continued right up to the glass door. Even in the middle of winter, the plants that hadn't dropped their leaves were casting faint green, wavering shade along the roads that morning.

But he wouldn't be passing under those trees today. Ryuuji kept going to the Zelkova tree-lined path. Though he didn't know whether Taiga had left the house without sleeping in, he was respecting her decision from the night before; he wouldn't go and wake her up in the morning.

The heavens must have been in an uproar... Well, he didn't know about that, but he really was happy about how Taiga was feeling. He had a lot of pretty complicated emotions about it. To be honest, he was lonely and felt a little like he had been left behind, but he was also just happy Taiga was thinking of him.

His breath was white as he walked under the leafless Zelkova trees by himself, deep in thought. Normally, when he walked this road with Taiga, he would be hit with her bag, verbally abused, strangled, blinded, or would have to deal with her being in a bad mood after being woken up too early or too late. He would be wailed at for her falling over, running into things, catching on things, for Kitamura-kun this or Minorin that, or because Dimhuahua and him had done something and grumble grumble. But then...but then, Taiga had made off on her own. She said it was for his sake and Minorin's.

Taiga really might have become an adult.

On the other hand, he was like this. She'd gained a lot of distance on him while he was bedridden from heartbreak and the flu. He should have been prepared the other night, but the same thoughts ran over and over in his head. *What should I do? What should I do? What should I do?*

"Hyah!"

Like Taiga had the other night, he slapped his own cheeks with both hands.

He really was at a standstill and didn't know what to do, but hadn't he decided he wouldn't run away? Then he needed to be serious about it. It was fine if he was embarrassed. That was all he could do. It was better than stagnating in place, unable to give up—anything would be better than that.

Ryuuji lifted his forehead to the cold midwinter wind and faced forward. Worrying about what kind of expression to make when he saw Minori wasn't something he needed to think about anymore.

He would get serious. He was at zero right now, but he could start again. That was it. He just had to make sure he didn't go into the negatives and not be too worried about Minori when he didn't need to be. It wasn't like he had been dumped by someone he was dating. She had just pointed out that they were at zero and that was that. From here, he could collect positive points again.

It had been unrequited love right from the start, after all.

He got to the intersection right as the lights turned green. He felt a little more energized at his slight luck. Ryuuji decided that if he saw Minori in the classroom, he would greet her first. He would do it with as loud a voice as he could, *Good morning!* After that, he didn't know whether the conversation would continue, but he would turn his own smile on her immediately after the break ended.

That was pretty much all he could do. At the very least, he could face forward and—

"Oh! Takasu-kun, good morning!"

God!

"Oh, hey, it's cold, isn't it?! Huh, where's Taiga? You're not with her?"

Ryuuji was now Takasu Zidane the second. He didn't know what that meant, but that was how it was. He did a spectacular Marseille Roulette as he slid right past the girl who was blocking his path at the end of the crosswalk. He passed by her like a whirlwind. Internally, he screamed, *I'm an idiiiiiooooot!*

He had walked without thinking right to the intersection where Taiga and Minori always waited for each other. He was really an idiot. If Taiga weren't awake yet, it was natural for *her* to be here. It should have been obvious Kushieda Minori would be there.

"W-wait! Takasu-kun!"

He wrapped himself in his scarf and pretended to snuffle. He pretended not to hear anything. The truth was that he could no longer turn around or stop of his own free will. With amazing speed, he kept going, unable to stop.

What had he been saying about greeting her?! What had he been saying about meeting her with a smile?! *Idiot, idiot, idiot, idiot, huge idiot. Die, you stupid damn idiot.* As he mentally abused himself, Ryuuji turned a deaf ear on Minori. He couldn't look at Minori's back, much less the expression on her face. He couldn't even look at the hem of her skirt. He couldn't even breathe in the air in a one-meter radius around where she existed.

"Heeey! Takasu-kun..."

He was on the verge of short-circuiting. Ryuuji's body froze up. At a loss for what to do, he walked with long strides. He turned his back harder than a rock to Minori's fading voice as he escaped for dear life. The drama of the amazing escape Inko-chan had made in the morning must have been foreshadowing this. Even as he had that silly thought, he couldn't face up to how terrible the thing he was doing was.

"Don't ruuuuuuun awaaaaay!"

It was no use telling him. Ryuuji quickened his pace to also run away from Taiga's voice from the night before, which echoed in his head.

"Why you baldo, Ryuuji, HRAAAAAAH! Don't you dare ruuuuuuuuuuuuuuun!"

I'm not balding...

Actually, Taiga's voice was echoing around him in a very realistic way, he thought.

"Oh, M-Minorin, good morning... GAAAAAAH!"

He turned at the terrible shriek at the same time as Minori did. A small idiot had fallen over in the middle of the crosswalk. It would have been fine if she had just fallen over, but she was in the blind spot of the approaching van.

Ryuuji and Minori threw their bags down at the same time and shot over.

What happened after that was in ominous slow motion.

Like a cat about to be hit, Taiga was frozen in front of the approaching tires. She couldn't move. Luckily, the van was slowing as Ryuuji jumped out in front of the windshield and clung to the glass. The surprised driver winced as he braked, and in that time, Minori grabbed Taiga's arm and hoisted her out of the road and onto the sidewalk.

"That was close, don't just jump out of nowhere, kid!" The driver's rough yell, the vibration of the engine, and the exhaust from the gas passed right by them.

Ryuuji's heart felt like it was going to burst, and his body trembled.

"Th-that was s-scary..."

"You idiot!" Ryuuji raised his voice without thinking.

"What do you think you're doing?! Seriously...!" Minori's voice cracked, too.

Sitting in the azalea bed with her duffel coat wide open, Taiga slowly looked at Ryuuji. She looked at Minori, too. Then in a small voice she said, "Sorry."

"Seriously! This isn't a joke! You were almost really run over!"

"Why did you jump out like that?! Here, stand up! Are you hurt?!"

Minori pulled Taiga up so she was finally standing upright. Minori dusted off the back of her dirty skirt by hitting it hard, and Taiga could only make a pitiful face.

"Look, fix up your coat, too! Put on your scarf! You're so sloppy about it... Oh!"

As she was rewrapping the fuchsia pink scarf she had finally bought for herself, Ryuuji noticed the scrapes on Taiga's palms. Without thinking, he grabbed and lifted her hands.

"You're bleeding!"

"She is! We need tissues!"

"I have some..." He raised his head and gulped as he swallowed his breath.

He noticed that Minori was looking at Taiga's hand, which he held, very closely. Taiga's hand trembled all the more. It seemed she had noticed, too. Minori pulled tissues out from her pocket and wiped at the cut. She held it.

It seemed that Minori had cut her hair slightly. The hair tips that sprung up at her chin seemed even more boyish than before. Under her bangs, her dark eyes lit up.

That was his limit.

Ryuuji turned around. He started walking and left Taiga and Minori behind. It might have seemed unnatural for him to do that, but he couldn't stay there any longer. He picked up his bag, which he had left by the sidewalk, and didn't even pat off the dirt as he once again ran from Minori for dear life. He didn't look at anything and didn't hear anything.

Taiga didn't yell at him to not run anymore. Under the pretense of putting his bag back on, Ryuuji turned around just slightly to look back at them. Minori had her back turned to him as she grabbed her own bag. Taiga was in the middle of the sidewalk, holding her head as she looked at the heavens. Her mouth opened and closed. *Klutz, klutz, klutz, klutz, klutz, I'm a klutz,* she was probably shouting without making a sound.

Yeah, you really are a klutz, Ryuuji agreed in a whisper. *You really aren't an adult. An adult wouldn't jump into the road and almost get hit by a car.*

Then, Ryuuji wanted to shout, too. *Idiot, idiot, idiot, idiot, idiot, I'm an idiot!* He wanted to turn to the heavens and wail.

Ahh, I would rather the school have burned down, he foolishly thought. He was close to tears as he ran away.

"**T**HE BEACH! The sun! Okinawa!"

"The poisonous snakes! Dr. Koto! Okinawa!"

BABAM! Two class trip permission slips were unveiled before Ryuuji's eyes as he came into the classroom. He pushed them away.

"What's with you all of a sudden...?"

Ryuuji's eyes narrowed into the shapes of crescents, harshly oozing out his unhappy mood. A normal person would have been in tears, but Noto and Haruta, who had developed a tolerance, looked fine as they lined their faces up chummily in front of him.

"What is it with you, Takasu? You're in a bad mood! Did you bring it? Did you bring this thing? The permission slip?!"

"Happy New Year! It's Okinawa! We're there five nights and six days and don't have to pay anything to go~! Whoo!"

It's not actually free... Ryuuji looked quietly back up at the naive idiot Haruta's face that year, too. Today, of all days, he was jealous of his friend's stupid face, which had no worries.

However, Haruta had mistaken his gaze for something else, and the color in his face changed. "Uh, what's wrong, Taka-chan? Stop it! My permission slip is for me!"

"I don't need that thing. I brought my own in already."

He really was jealous.

Ryuuji's lips stayed pinched together as he put his bag on his seat. He was aware that his bad mood, which he couldn't play off as anything else, had caused Noto and Haruta to exchange looks, but he couldn't explain it to them. He couldn't get himself to tell them that he had been heartbroken ever since Kushieda Minori, who could walk into the classroom at any moment, had rejected him on Christmas Eve. He also couldn't tell them that just a few minutes earlier, when Minori brightly greeted him as though nothing had changed, he'd completely ignored her and run away.

He sat at his seat and held his head in his hands. The more he recalled it, the more he felt like he had done something petty. In the end, wasn't he the worst? Even though he had been rejected, wasn't it pretty much only the worst scum who would so obviously ignore someone like that?

It was petty and the worst and made him scum... He was already feeling terrible, but he was sure he had unnecessarily deepened his wounds even further. If he kept this up, he would keep falling into the negatives, and she'd start hating him.

"Ahhhh...whoa...fwhoa!"

"Hey! Hey!" Noto pulled away Ryuuji's hands, which he was using to tear at his hair. "Takasu, what're you grumbling about? What's actually gotten into you? Did something happen? Oh, are you just feeling off from the aftereffects of the flu?"

"Actually, that was a shock. I couldn't believe it when we asked you to go start-of-year shrine visiting, and you were like, 'I just got back from being hospitalized, so I can't go.' But look, maybe you'll feel better after seeing this! I'm suuuper excited about the trip, so I went ahead and bought this! Whoo~! Take a look at it!"

His hands, which had been holding his head, were slapped to the side. Ryuuji had a book thrust right in front of his face. What Haruta was showing him proudly was a guidebook. Despite of himself, Ryuuji found his eyes glued to the cover, which had a picture and text that read, "The Complete Guide to Okinawa!"

The shining sun. The deep blue sky. The green, glittering coral reef. The beach that was so white it looked fake. Young people in swimsuits were smiling as the wind ruffled their hair. The boys and girls were in the water up to their knees and holding each other's shoulders in a friendly way...and they each even held a giant pineapple in their hands!

"Aha ha ha ha ha!"

He started to laugh. The corners of his eyes started to water. He wasn't sad, just done in by the ridiculous juxtaposition of the beautiful scene and his current state.

The people in the picture were bright, brilliant, and really did look like they were having fun. He was like the shadow that would form under their feet. It was funny. It was actually hilarious.

Ryuuji didn't know how Noto had interpreted that laughter, but he relaxed. Like an otter that had captured a small fish in its hands, Noto laughed, too. "Ehee hee!" It was so uncute, it was irritating.

"Aren't you so looking forward to it?! This blue ocean! We're so lucky that we get to go to Okinawa for a school trip! My old junior high buddy is going to Kyoto and Nara for his high school trip, and we went there during junior high, too! Like, you can only take so many temples and shrines!"

"Hee hee, how cruel! There's this one place I definitely want to go to in Okinawa! Cape Mambo!"

He probably means Cape Manzamo... Ryuuji thought distantly.

"And also the US bases! Look, don't they look cool?! The mariners!"

You mean marines...and normal people can't get into the bases anyway, Ryuuji thought even more distantly. Regardless, he didn't have the strength to make fun of Haruta.

"Aim and fire!" Haruta said, and finally Noto stopped. "You've got the wrong idea of Okinawa."

"Yo, morning! You're already looking at Okinawa guidebooks! You're so eager to do your homework!"

They turned at the energetic voice that was so obviously that of an athlete and put up their hands in greeting. "Yo." The boy whose friendly eyes squinted from behind his glasses as he raised his hand in reply was the student council vice president and class rep, Kitamura Yuusaku.

"Takasu, I heard you had the flu at the end of the year? That must have been tough. Are you okay now?"

"Uh...yeah..."

"What is it? What happened? You don't seem like you're doing great. Hah! Your high fever couldn't have..."

Wrinkles appeared on Kitamura's forehead as he looked fervently and intently in the vicinity of Ryuuji's crotch. Ryuuji crossed his legs and guarded himself from the stare.

"Yo, master. Are you doing it this year, too? This thing."

Noto hit his hands together twice and bowed his head. What he was indicating with that gesture was, of course...

"You mean being the Patron Saint of Broken Hearts? Of course I am! I'm going to get a firm grip on the students' hearts this year, too! I'll appeal to people with my new persona and save the brokenhearted from the darkness of... What's wrong, Takasu? Why are you looking at me?"

"Nothing..."

Ryuuji shook his head in a fluster. He averted his eyes from Kitamura's, which were about twice as big and more defined than Noto's. *Oh, no.* He had reacted without thinking to the keyword "brokenhearted."

"It's just, there are issues with continuing the Patron Saint of Broken Hearts broadcast program... We've started to run out of brokenhearted guests. We've finished with the student council members and even gone through the softball underclassmen... If we keep going like this, the program will be in trouble."

"Can't you prepare some plants for that? Oh, look, I already found a good candidate!"

Ryuuji looked where Noto pointed and then closed his eyes. "Whoa!" He turned his face down and gripped his knees until his nails turned white. He wanted to run. He wanted to just get away, but...

"Yo, Kushieda! You cut your hair, didn't you?! You must have had a heartbreak?! Come be on Kitamura's broken hearts radio show!"

"Huh? Kushieda, is that why you cut your hair? You barely cut it, so it's hard to even tell. If you're gonna do it, be more daring about trimming it back. Make it like the bald cap I gave you! Right, Taka-chan?!"

Haruta had latched right on to his back, and he couldn't run...

Ryuuji lifted his eyes. He gritted his back teeth and stole a glance. Taking off her tartan-checked scarf, Minori spoke as brightly as usual, like she had forgotten all about Ryuuji just ignoring her.

"You boys are so loud! Could you keep out of people's heads?! Pervy wervy one touchy!"

Hey, we've got an idiot here, that's an idiot. Noto and Haruta pointed at Minori as they laughed at her. Even Kitamura got carried along and laughed with abandon as he stretched out his arms.

"You're always welcome if you got your heart broken! Come jump into my arms! And then go on the radio!"

"You got it, master! Of course you've got a swole chest!"

"Pheew! Kushieda's heartbroken! Pheew~!"

Ryuuji felt a twinge.

He was glad it wasn't tears. It was just the taste of iron coming from his lips from biting too hard. Left out of the joke, he still couldn't even look at Minori's face.

"Tch, let's go, Taiga. Those guys really are giant idiots! They don't know that this haircut cost four thousand five hundred yen!"

Minori put her arm over Taiga's shoulder and turned her around. Taiga nodded as she looked up at Minori, clinging to Minori's waist like a koala. "This is how you steal a million!" she said over her shoulder.

Maybe because it was the new semester, or because of Okinawa, or both, but on that day, the boys (Ryuuji excluded) were reckless and in high spirits.

"Right, right, you could have Tiger as a plant, too! Kitamura, have her on the radio with you!"

"Hee hee hee, you're right! Nice idea! Now, jump into my chest, Tiger~!"

Haruta pulled open Kitamura's school jacket from behind. It wasn't like there was anything to see but a long-sleeved shirt...

"Don't go, Taiga! That's a trap Kitamura's made!" With both her hands, Minori was covering Taiga's eyes firmly.

"Ow! Minorin, that hurts!"

"You mustn't look. I've gotten tricked by that trap once! You think it's not a big deal, and then while you're looking at it, something black and unthinkable appears!"

Ha ha ha. Kitamura laughed with abandon with his jacket still open. "Hey, hey, that just sounds bad. When exactly did I show you some black thing?"

"In the summer! At Ahmin's villa!"

Did that really happen? Kitamura tilted his head lightly.

"Oh my! Oh dear!" Haruta, who had been holding open Kitamura's jacket, had found something on his long-sleeved shirt. He brought his face closer and strained his eyes.

"Wait, wait a sec! You idiot master Kitamura! You've got food all over yourself right here. How embarrassing~! Hey, Taka-chan, what kind of stains do you think these are~?"

"What did you say?!" Ryuuji reflexively stood up on hearing the word "stain."

"Here and here," Haruta pointed them out. He really did see the shadow of two circles on Kitamura's chest. He observed them meticulously. Was it sauce or soy sauce? They were in the same position his nipples would be, and the longer he looked at them, the more they really did look like nipples—

"Those are just his nipples!"

Ryuuji choked. How dirty. He wanted to pull out his eyeballs, which had so diligently looked at those things, and wash them out with palm detergent. In a fluster, Kitamura pulled together the front of his jacket. His cheeks were red.

"Oh no! I forgot to wear a T-shirt underneath!"

"I'm out!" Minori arched her body backward, arms crossed in front of her.

Quickly slipping over next to Taiga, Noto poked her in the elbow. Out of all things he could have uttered, he said, "Hey! This is so lucky, Tiger! So lucky!"

"What is??"

Even someone who wasn't Taiga would want to say that. Then, even Haruta immediately came to stand on his knees beside Taiga and suddenly opened the guidebook to show it to her.

"Tiger, read this part!"

"Huh?! H-hentai!"

"Hyaah! Bwa ha ha~! What? Did you hear that just now~?! I thought that might be how she'd read it~!"

Haruta still had the "Must Know Okinawan Words!" feature open to the *"Haitai!"* section. He probably had a death wish. At that moment, blood spurted up from Taiga's eyes—no, not really. Ryuuji just felt bloodthirsty intent emanating from her.

Taiga grabbed Noto's thumb with her right hand and Haruta's with her left, and then lowered her hips. "HYAH!" she yelled. As if through some kind of sorcery, she sent Noto and Haruta somersaulting up into the air past each other. They hit the floor on their backs and couldn't move. They were probably dead.

Then, Taiga raised her face and said a single word, incredibly loudly. *"Haitai!"*

Minori grinned. "You've done it!"

Kitamura was still shyly holding his chest.

Unable to follow the series of skits being enacted before him, Ryuuji could only stand there, dumbfounded. Without thinking, he lifted his eyes and looked at Minori, who was standing next to him.

It took him by surprise.

He felt like he had been happy-go-luckily crossing a wooden bridge, only to suddenly glimpse a muddy stream under his feet between the slats. Something Ryuuji didn't need to think about came to his mind.

It was good that everyone was having fun. It was just, how could Minori act like everything was normal the way she was doing right now? How could she be bright and unchanged from usual when he—the person she had just rejected—was right in front of her eyes?

Was it that, to Minori, that event—that event that had happened not even two weeks ago—was something she could easily forget? Nothing more than a trifling accident?

"..."

His breath caught.

Maybe noticing Ryuuji's gaze, Minori also lifted her head. Their gazes collided, but immediately, Minori's usual smile formed on her face. "What's up with you?" she whispered in a slightly jokey tone.

It seemed she'd already forgotten that Ryuuji had ignored her—she had forgotten Ryuuji's low and scummy behavior.

That was his limit. Ryuuji pried his eyes off of her, then turned his back to Minori and started running away. He went by himself at a high speed away from his circle of friends. In a situation like this, it seemed that the too-sensitive, awkward, rejected boy could only go hide in the bathroom.

"Oh, this is perfect timing! Takasu-kun, do you remember me?!"

When he headed toward the door, he noticed a boy he didn't recall peeking into the classroom from the hallway and waving at him.

"Look, I was the guy wearing the bear kigurumi at the Christmas Eve student council party, and—"

"Oh, right, when that happened..."

He remembered. On Christmas Eve, Ryuuji had made a proposition to some guy in a bear outfit, to the effect of "Would you trade clothes with me?!" They had traded his suit for the bear. So much had happened afterward that he completely pushed it from his memory. Ryuuji bowed his head in a fluster.

"Sorry, I completely forgot. Thanks for coming all the way over here."

"No, whenever is fine with me. I just got mine from a party store. More importantly, this suit looked super expensive, so my mom told me to hurry up and give it back."

"Oh, you even got it dry cleaned... Thank you so much, really, I'm really sorry."

Ryuuji received the suit, which was still in the plastic bag from the cleaners, and once again bowed his head. *Oh no, oh no.*

He still needed to get the bear suit over to the cleaners and properly repay him.

"More importantly, here's this. It was in the pocket, but you didn't get in any trouble because of that, did you? I looked around for you, but I couldn't find you anywhere."

"Oh..."

The guy handed the small, wrapped box apologetically to Ryuuji, and a current ran through Ryuuji's hand. This was the Christmas present he had planned to give Minori while confessing to her.

Ryuuji took it and replied, "No, it's fine. This is... I just didn't need it on that day."

He shook his head back and forth and, in his mind, added, *Really*.

Really, I didn't need this. Even if he'd had it, he probably wouldn't have been able to give it to her, anyway.

"I see. Oh, that's a relief! Actually, I was a little scared of coming here. I was like, what'll I do if Takasu-kun is actually a delinquent? Murase and the others said that you're 'Really a normal and good guy, so it's okay.' So it's true."

Ryuuji looked down. It was true he wasn't a delinquent, but he didn't know whether he was really a good guy anymore. Was a guy who ignored the person who rejected him actually good? He was definitely a petty guy, at the very least.

He asked the boy's name one last time, promised that he would return the bear outfit, and watched as the seemingly agreeable person, who appeared to be friends with Murase from the student council, left.

The contents of the present left behind in his hand was a hairpin that he picked out two weeks ago. It had been at a random goods store. The girl at the shop had looked terrified by him as he hemmed and hawed and persevered to pick it out.

He thought that a one-thousand-yen hairpin might be a little too dull, but he didn't want to get her a weirdly grand gift when they weren't even dating. He also remembered that Minori had been tying up her bangs, which got in her way while they were taking their tests. He thought a pen case or pouch might do, but rather than something practical, he felt like giving her something that glittered and would be pretty. Even if it was cheap, it was fitting for Christmas night, and he wanted to get her something beautiful.

I'll throw it away.

That's what he thought. *I'll throw this away immediately.*

It was almost a subconscious instinct, but he didn't want to put this thing, which was connected to the difficult memory of that night, in his own pocket.

He tried to throw it into a trash bin without thinking, but his hands stopped. He clicked his tongue and roughly pulled off the unnecessary Christmas tree-print wrapping paper. Was he really separating the trash at a time like this...? He was; he couldn't help it. He opened the box and pulled out the properly wrapped hairpin. He crumpled the ribbon on the packaging he no longer needed and threw it into the burnables section of the trash. It was unnecessary wrapping and annoying.

Ryuuji grabbed the incombustible hairpin. He looked at it with his sanpaku eyes without reservation. It was large and silver, with a wavy pattern. It had transparent, gold, and orange glittering glass beads in a pattern that made them look like splashing bubbles.

He thought that it looked like something that suited Minori. Among the hairpins of many colors and many different shapes, this one suited her the best. He thought that she could wear it during class, at softball club, and when she was working. When she would put it on, she could remember him. Whenever he saw her wearing it, he would feel like his feelings had gotten through to her.

But he hadn't given it to her. He didn't need it anymore.

"Save me, Taka-chan~! Look at this! Tiger bit me! Here's the proof! Look at those bite marks!"

"It's because you keep saying *haitai haitai haitai* and won't stop! What's with you, you long haired bug?! I'll exterminate you! We've got to get rid of you for the sake of the planet!"

Haruta, mid-squabble with Taiga, ran into Ryuuji's back like a tattling kid. Taiga, who was following, also came over. The two of them noticed the hairpin in Ryuuji's hand at the same time, but Haruta was first to respond.

"Huh? What's that thing? What are you doing with it?"

Taiga groaned a little. *Ah.* He had told her he had bought Minori a hairpin. She glanced at the trash, saw the clearly Christmas-themed wrapping paper, and seemed to understand what it was. Taiga was generally oblivious, but at times like these, she could be tactful.

"This is, well, what can I say...? I don't need it..."

"Huh, you don't need it?! Then give it to me! Look, I kind of feel like my bangs are getting in the way!"

Haruta, who had no clue about anything, took the hairpin, put it on his bangs, and posed. "How's it look?!"

This had gone quite differently than Ryuuji imagined. He stared in melancholy at his friend, who looked so bad with the hairpin that it made him nauseated.

"G-give it back!"

"Ow ow ow?! Wait, what, why?!"

"It doesn't matter, just give it back! Give it back! Give it back! Give it back! Give it baaack!"

Jumping onto Haruta's back, Taiga climbed the tall idiot like a tree and tried to extract the hairpin from his long hair. "Gyaa~!" Haruta shrieked.

"That's—still—Ryuuji's! Just hurry up and give it back—"

The door opened and the homeroom teacher appeared, carrying the attendance record in one hand. Several hairs from Haruta's head were sacrificed, pulled right out along with the hairpin.

"It burned down!"

Huh? The students of class 2-C could only look uneasily at Koigakubo Yuri, the bachelorette (age 30) standing at the teacher's platform.

The bachelorette (age 30) said "Thank you! Thank you!" as she took the permission slips that Kitamura had gathered, stacked them together, quickly put them into an envelope, and sandwiched it under her arm with the attendance sheet. Then she looked around at the students' faces with an unspeakably iffy smile.

"It burned down. It's unfortunate. Um, but, we won't cancel it. So, well, um, it's fine. It is. It'll go on as planned. Okay?"

"Teach...we don't get what you're saying at all. Please be clearer."

At Kitamura's completely reasonable words, the bachelorette (age 30) seemed to have given up on deceiving them.

"It's the hotel!"

As though fortifying herself, she raised her voice in a teacher-like way.

"It's the hotel that we should have stayed at for the trip in Okinawa! It burned down during an end-of-the-year fire! There are no longer any hotels that can accommodate all one hundred and sixty-eight second years in Okinawa! So, we can't go to Okinawa anymore! But, the trip isn't canceled! We'll just have a slightly compact two-night three-day mountain ski trip instead! Isn't that great?!"

WHAAAAAAAAAAAAAAAAAAAAAA?!

At almost exactly the same time, they heard a terrible scream, similar to a shriek, from the classroom next door. *GAAAAAH! GYAAAAH!* They heard unknowable despair from a class, somewhere, that made even the ceiling shake and quiver.

"No waaaay?! Seriously?"

"This is the worst! It's so so so terrible!"

"WAAAAAAAAH! It would have been my first time on a plane and my first time in Okinawaaaaaaa!"

"Why are we going to a mountain in the middle of winter?! Are you trying to make us upset?!"

"Skiing is fun, too," the bachelorette (age 30) followed up. "A ski slope with powdered snow floating around! A silvery-white snow scene! Two people drawing a heart with their ski tracks! And then everyone going 'yahoo!'"

"I don't want that! It's too dull! This is our once-in-a-lifetime trip!"

"This isn't a joke! I'm definitely going to Okinawa! I don't care when it happens, please make it Okinawa!"

"That's right! I don't want to go to a mountain in the winter! Let's all boycott it!"

At that radical opinion, the class started applauding in agreement. However, the bachelorette (age 30) glanced at the envelope under her arm.

"But we've already received your permission slips...so we're going ahead as planned..."

The students started screaming in agony.

Haruta, who had been so excited he bought a guidebook, began to weep. Kitamura must have wanted to go to Okinawa, too, because he grew agitated at their homeroom teacher. "I decisively object! This is nonsense!"

The girls attacked with foul mouths. "Screw off!"

"This is unreasonable!"

"Old maid!"

"Thirty year old!"

Even Taiga, the little lady who could probably go to Okinawa whenever she wanted, hit her desk over and over in protest.

With severe resistance raining down on her whole body, the pitiful bachelorette (age 30) had a troubled look on her face. "It's not like I burned down the hotel in Okinawa."

That was probably true.

Among the people in uproar, Ryuuji, alone, had become the inhabitant of another world. His two lizard-like eyes opened wide. It wasn't the bachelorette (age 30) who had burned down the hotel.

If anything, it was him.

As he had come to school, his curse, "Burn and disappear!" had traveled through the air as sparks to the Okinawan hotel, just as his words had intended.

Ryuuji apologized in his heart to his classmates, who spilled tears and continued to protest. In that moment, he felt like the shrieking cries of a snowstorm on a winter mountain were more appropriate for him than Okinawa's blinding sunlight. The curse had been successful and, though unfortunate, Ryuuji was actually really relieved. He absolutely did not want to go to a blue ocean and blue sky. He wasn't in the frame of mind to smile brightly in the sun.

The shadowy overcast sky. The continually falling snow. The soaking-damp underwear. The incredibly smelly rental skiwear. The bears. The avalanches. The locked-room murders. That was good.

Unbeknownst to anyone, the cursed ship blew its shrill whistle. The ghostly crew sneakily chuckled to themselves. Ryuuji was fine with that. Actually, he didn't even care about the school trip. He didn't care whether they were confined on the cold winter mountain or ended up playing tag in a maze of sewer pipes, or journeyed to the land of the dead. A once-in-a-lifetime school trip? Why would he care about something like that?

"Damn it! Why is Ami-chan late on today of all days?!"

"Ami-chan wouldn't stay silent about something like this!"

"Ami-chan would have done something!"

Come to think of it, the black-hearted model hadn't shown herself. The guys started baying, "Ami-chaaan! Ami-chaaan!" into the void.

However, the bachelorette (age 30) simply said, "Kawashima-san is in Hawaii for work. Her plane home didn't make it on time, so she's taking today off. But look, she's already gone to a tropical island, so wouldn't she prefer a winter mountain?! Hee hee!"

"Of course not!"

The bachelorette (age 30) gave up any further resistance to the uncontrollable state of affairs. She turned her back to the students and headed toward the blackboard. There, she wrote distinctly: "Life doesn't go the way you want it!!"

"Oh!"

Without thinking, Ryuuji let out a loud exclamation. *Really?* he thought. *She's already back?*

He had gone out grocery shopping for dinner as the sky began darkening into dusk. The midwinter wind was sharp as a knife, and the people coming and going along the street were quickly hurrying home.

Ryuuji had caught sight of a certain incredibly attention-gathering form while he was peeking into a bookstore before going to the supermarket. The tall person he was looking at from over the bookshelves was definitely Kawashima Ami.

She stood among the people lined up in front of the racks of women's magazines. Though she was tall, her face was delicate. Her pale profile, adorned with giant sunglasses that glittered with an Armani logo, traced a beautiful line from her nose to her chin. She'd messily tied up her silky, shiny straight hair, exposing her neck. She was wearing a down jacket that was probably expensive enough to make Ryuuji want to die. She wore old-looking jeans, stuffed into her boots, and though she wasn't wearing heels, her legs were still terrifyingly long. With her Chanel bag, she seemed to give off an oppressive aura that shouted, "There's a beauty here! I'm a model!"

Ami-chan-sama, whom he hadn't seen in so long, looked just as she always did.

When they had last parted, during the Christmas Eve party, it had been pretty awkward. It was as though Ami had gotten fed up with Ryuuji's foolishness and gone home alone. He hadn't noticed Taiga had left, and he had believed like a kid that the world would conveniently align itself... He really had been pretty foolish that day. There had been too much going on for him to call out to Ami as she left. It was only natural that she'd be fed up with him.

Ami definitely predicted the situation he was currently in, even though he had thought she was just saying stuff that made her seem like she knew more than she did. Ami might have known what kind of outcome Ryuuji's foolishness would invite. Her words were always painful, but that was probably because they were the pointed truth.

"..."

Surprised, he lowered his head into the cooking book he was skimming where he stood.

Ami was approaching him from the women's magazine corner. She was listening to music on an iPod and seemed not to have noticed Ryuuji's presence at all.

Ryuuji froze up, unable to awkwardly raise his head and say something at that point. Quite unexpectedly, Ami advanced closer and closer into the cooking book corner and reached out a hand to grab a magazine right in front of Ryuuji's eyes. *Staple Hot Meals: Brown Rice Bento* was apparently her goal.

"Sorr...oh."

Ryuuji blinked.

The moment she pulled out the magazine, Ami's Chanel bag hit Ryuuji's hand. Ryuuji dropped the magazine, and Ami finally noticed him as she apologized. He couldn't see her expression hidden behind her glasses, but she seemed about to say "Oh" as her mouth formed a pout.

"Don't bother with that. The Staple Hot Meals series is completely unusable." Ryuuji's voice grumbled from the awkwardness, but he still tried to speak as normally as he could.

"Tch!" Ami acknowledged Ryuuji's existence by clicking her tongue. She placed the magazine she had pulled out back on the shelf, contorting her mouth provokingly.

I feel something vividly evil!

The moment Ami tried to turn on her heel, her bag caught on the boring cell-phone keychain that protruded from Ryuuji's down jacket. Ami turned around, shook her bag vigorously in order to get it back, and held it to her chest with exaggerated movements.

"What do you think you're trying to do to my Chanel bag?!"

"What are you trying to do to me?!"

At the terrifying look Ami gave him through her sunglasses, Ryuuji accidentally showed his demonic face, which would have caused a shudder of fear in anyone. The sudden argument that had started between the beautiful model and murder-faced boy got them looks from everyone around. However, Ami didn't mind that at all.

"Ugh, you're so annoying! Actually, why are you even here? Disappear for me, would you?"

She was really unbelievably rude. *Whaaat?!* Ryuuji's face contorted even further.

"What did you say?! Actually, what's up with your attitude?! I-I was just—"

I got rejected by Minori on Christmas Eve! He couldn't say that, of course...

"I was just hospitalized with the flu, you know! I had a fever of 40 degrees Celsius, and I wasn't even conscious! I can't believe your conscience would let you attack me with that attitude!"

"How should I have known?! Actually, you had a 40-degree fever? Then..."

Ami whipped off her sunglasses and nibbled on their end as wrinkles formed on her forehead. She narrowed her pretty, double-lidded eyes and stared at Ryuuji's crotch.

"..."

"Could you mind your own business?! My genes are still alive!"

Ryuuji crossed his legs and went on the defensive. As expected from childhood friends, Ami and Kitamura's vulgar circuit of thoughts was surprisingly similar.

"Oh, really. Huh, good for you. Well, bye."

Ami carelessly stuck her sunglasses into the back pocket of her jeans. With a smile on her lips that was easy to recognize as manufactured, she turned her back coldly on him.

There was a dark whirlpool whipping around in Ryuuji's mind. *What a girl...* How could her unpleasantness even be described? She was irritating. He knew she had an ugly personality.

He knew about her two-faced, twisted nature, too. Regardless, he was still shocked. The way she treated him was absurd. Why in the world did she have to take an attitude like that with him? Was it because she was fed up with him? Even if that was it, wasn't this too much?

"Hey, wait! Why did you take up that fighting stance all of a sudden?!"

"Oh, you want me to give it to you straight? Then I'll tell you. I don't like you anymore, Takasu-kun."

"Wha...at?!"

She put it so simply that it couldn't be misinterpreted. Ryuuji stood there, dumbfounded, in spite of himself.

"Wh...why?!"

"Huh? Don't follow me. You're seriously so annoying."

"Did you really...hate me that much...?"

"Ow! What do you think you're doing? Don't screw around with me!"

He was so shocked, he'd unintentionally reached out his arm, knocking the ecobag that contained his wallet and phone against Ami's butt. Blocking the aisle of the bookstore, showered in stares, Ami pointed at Ryuuji and said, "You want me to spell it out for you?! I hate you because you're an idiot!"

"Bwah! She said she hates him cause he's stupid...ha ha ha!"

He heard merciless laughter, turned, and saw the owner of the voice. *Ha ha ha!* The person continuing to laugh at other people's business was short, had her fluffy hair tied loosely to the side, wore a multicolor knit hat and a long, flower-patterned skirt, and had boots peeking from the hem of her white angora coat. In other words, it was Taiga.

"You're so slow!" said Ami. "It's already ten minutes past the time we were supposed to meet!"

"Don't pick at the details. You're a Dimhuahua—you can't even tell the time."

"I can so!"

Ryuuji was surprised by the conversation that was happening over his head. Was it possible that these natural born enemies, who had fought blood for blood for so long, in a rare moment in the history of the world, were friendly and meeting each other in a bookstore on the street?

"Here, this was 14 dollars. That makes it 40."

"Uhh...so if one dollar is about one hundred yen..."

Ryuuji unintentionally sighed as he watched Taiga clumsily pull out and count one thousand yen bills from her cat wallet.

"At what point did you two get close enough to exchange gifts?"

"These aren't gifts. I'm paying Dimhuahua back. I only have ten thousand yen bills! Give me change!"

"Whaat?! Aren't you supposed to have this already prepared, considering you're the one who asked me to buy this for you?" As she muttered, Ami also pulled out her Dior wallet and the two of them finished exchanging money. Then, Ami glanced at Ryuuji's face.

"Tch..."

She scowled and clicked her tongue. The why-are-you-still-here aura exuded from her whole body. Ryuuji tried to prod the shins of Ami's boots under the table with the tips of his shoes but accidentally kicked Taiga.

"Ow! Was that you just now?!"

She glared at him, and he turned away. He tried to bury his expression, but he was immediately found out.

"It was you!"

She returned the favor by stepping on his feet.

"Welcome to Sudoh-bucks!" the female college student's welcoming voice rang out. If the actual store they were ripping off knew what was going on, the café would have been in dire straits.

After meeting in the bookstore, the three of them had set up camp in the Pseudobucks, aka Sudoh Coffee Stand and Bar's nonsmoking section, as usual. Jazz music streamed through the store. Taiga ordered a giant bowl of café au lait and pancakes, Ryuuji had the house blend, and Ami had a café latte. Sitting next to Taiga, Ryuuji couldn't get himself to look at Ami, who was right in front of him and not hiding her obvious irritation (she hated him because he was stupid, after all).

"So what did you get Ami to buy you?" he said.

Even though he wasn't really interested, he peeked into the paper bag Taiga had received. If it was 14 and 40 dollars, then it was within an acceptable price range, he thought gloomily.

"A pouch and sandals! They were in a magazine, and it said that they only had them in Hawaii! Hee hee, it's this!" Taiga pulled out a waterproof pouch decorated with dancing hula girls and casual sandals made with natural materials.

"Oh, right... In the end, these things were wasted... Ahh, I was so looking forward to it though. Oh well, I guess I can use these normally once it's summer."

Lifting her face from her cup of café latte, Ami's eyes went round with curiosity. "What? Why are they wasted? Aren't you bringing them on the school trip to Okinawa? Why can't you? They're perfect for that. I even went and looked for the ones you specifically asked me for. Gosh, you're just so—"

"Oh right, you don't know yet, Dimhuahua. The school trip has turned into a two-night, three-day ski trip."

"What?!" Ami's café latte cup clattered against its saucer.

"The hotel burned down. So, we're being locked up on this suuuuper cold winter mountain."

"What?! Seriously?! Whaaaat~?! No way, you can't be serious?! But I bought shorts and T-shirts and stuff for Okinawa! Actually, what do they mean we're only staying two nights?! Isn't that short?! And they're making us ski, too?! I hate this so much!"

"Sorry..."

"Why are you apologizing, Takasu-kun?"

"Why are you saying sorry?"

Unable to reply to the two of them, Ryuuji sipped his coffee with distant eyes. On top of already being hated just because, if he said, "It burned down because I cursed it," he didn't know how they would look at him.

Ami put up her hands. Currently in a situation where she didn't need to put on her goody-two-shoes mask, she contorted her mouth and spat poison.

"Ughh, I said not to screw around with me... Actually, this is the pits! Why have we got to ski on a school trip? I just don't get it at all. It's seriously so so so irritating! Ahh, maybe I can skip if I say I have work!"

"If you want to skip it you can, but I have one thing to say to you about the trip." Taiga slowly thrust her body over the table, sounding serious. "Oh!" The end of the ribbon on the chest of her dress dipped into her café au lait, and a flustered Ryuuji hurried to rescue it.

"It's so important that I went out of my way to ask you to meet me outside of school. Ryuuji was here by coincidence, but this is really convenient, so it's good."

Taiga glanced at Ryuuji. Not knowing what she meant, Ryuuji was taking emergency measures to rub coffee off Taiga's ribbon. He pushed the café au lait bowl far off, so she wouldn't make the same mistake, and didn't notice Ami looking at him with exasperation in her eyes.

Taiga narrowed her eyes slightly, however. She turned to Ami and declared, "We lost Okinawa, but a school trip is a school trip. It'll last in your memories, and it's not much different from a big event. Because of that, Dimhuahua, I'll tell you this straight.

If you come, please make sure you definitely don't hang around Ryuuji."

"Huh? Are you trying to say *I'm* the one who's hanging around *him* and causing problems?"

Lovingly clutching her Chanel bag to her chest, Ami glared at Ryuuji with hatred. *But wait a second,* he wanted to say. It wasn't as though Ryuuji had asked Taiga to say that, so even if she glared at him like that, he didn't know what the intent behind Taiga's remark was. Ryuuji sipped at his coffee to calm himself.

"Ryuuji likes Minorin."

"Bweeeeh!"

"Ew, Ryuuji, that's gross."

Cough! Sputter! Ryuuji held a napkin up to his choking mouth. *What are you saying?!* He looked up at Taiga with tears in his eyes.

"Huuh..."

Across from him, looking at him like a devilish snake that had spotted prey would, Ami's pretty face raised itself up dramatically. Her lips, glittering with gloss, contorted. For the first time that day and that year, her eyes sparkled with glee as she surveyed the state of affairs.

Ryuuji's face turned red as he choked. He looked exactly like a terrifying hungry ghost from hell as he looked back at Ami.

"And Minorin also likes Ryuuji."

"Hmmm..."

"What?! Wait...wait a second! Is that what you think?!"

"Just keep quiet. I know she definitely does... I just know. But there's a lot of things going on, so they're having a hard time getting together. I won't let anyone get in the way anymore. Even you, Dimhuahua. That's what I've decided."

Taiga had had her say.

Ami looked at Taiga's face, scooped up the foam of her café au lait with her teaspoon, and licked it with the tip of her tongue. For just a moment, she checked Ryuuji's expression with a glance.

"I see. Well, I've heard what you've had to say, but...why are you coming to me with this now? Why are you suddenly saying this?"

"Ryuuji got rejected by Minorin on Christmas Eve!"

Nooooo! His mouth formed a noiseless scream and he writhed in agony, but there was no one to notice.

"Seriously?"

"Yeah! He got rejected!"

Ami blinked. A couple at the table next to them turned to look at them. Even the owner of the café, Sudoh-san, had popped his head over the counter. *Rejected?! Who?! That kid with the scary face?! That delinquent kid?! How sad!* As he heard the overlapping, inconsiderate whispers, Ryuuji's heart was stabbed at from all sides.

He wanted to drown himself in the sea that was his house blend coffee. Ryuuji covered his head and leaned down on the table but then used the last of his strength to raise his face.

"What actually happened was that Kushieda rejected me by telling me not to confess on Christmas Eve before I could even confess!"

It was certainly true that he had been rejected by Minori, but why did Taiga have to go spreading that around? If he could, he would have pretended as though it had never happened. What was he going to do now that she had shared the memory with others? And why Kawashima Ami, out of all people?

"Huuuh. I see..."

At Ami's sweetly nasal voice, which was filled with poison, Ryuuji raised his head. She was probably going to say something terrible to him, the guy she hated for being stupid. She could say whatever she wanted. He was already riddled with wounds. Even if he got one or two more cuts, it wouldn't change anything.

However, at that moment, Ami's gaze shifted away from Ryuuji's face. Her mouth contorted into a line, as if she'd tried to smile but failed at it. She hid her expression with her café latte cup, and in a tone of voice like she was talking to herself, muttered, "So you've already been deeply hurt..."

Then, for some reason, her gaze went to Taiga instead of Ryuuji.

Taiga, who was holding her café au lait bowl with both hands, noticed her gaze and raised her eyes.

"The school trip is the last event for Ryuuji and Minorin to become honest with each other—I think it's a special opportunity. So, I don't want anyone to get in the way. Do you get that? Do you?"

Suddenly, she looked at Ryuuji.

"It would have been a lot better if it had been Okinawa, but we don't have time to talk about luxuries. 'Life doesn't go the way you want it,' after all. So I don't care whether it's a ski resort or a gloomy mountain. I want to see what Minorin's real feelings are. It's our best and last chance. It's our last chance because we're choosing different classes. Ryuuji's taking the science course, right?"

"Yeah... That's what I'm hoping."

"Minori is going into the humanities. We'll be in different classes, and you'll be separated within the year. If you're rejected even when you're in the same class, what'll happen when you're in different classes? This school trip really is the last chance! You got that?"

She stared up at him, and Ryuuji gulped a little. The following year, they'd be in different classes—another reality that he couldn't change. His heart was easily moved by the thought of his adolescence being broken up.

I got to be in the same class as Kushieda-san! So much time already passed since that spring, when he had been so delighted. This was a crucial moment: he could just abandon the race or keep running even though he was behind by a lap.

"So, Dimhuahua! You're okay with that?! I want you to stop teasing Ryuuji and clinging all over him!"

"Oh really? Did I ever cling all over Takasu-kun? I don't remember?"

"Ever since you appeared in our world, you've been clinging to Ryuuji, and it's depressing!"

"Was I? Well, I don't really care either way."

As though teasing Taiga, Ami put on her goody-two-shoes smile. Then she suddenly muttered in a low voice, "If that's actually what you want."

She put on her sunglasses to hide her eyes as she said that. It seemed Taiga hadn't completely heard what she said. Still expressionless, she finished up the last of her pancake in one bite.

Ami, however, didn't say it again. She slowly finished drinking her water, looked at the time, and stretched. Then she checked her cell phone before putting on her down coat and Chanel bag.

"Ahh, this smells of stupid. That was such a useless conversation. I'm not interested in your cheap love lives, so please do whatever you want. Well, I'm going home soon. I'm still feeling out of it from the jet lag. Are you guys staying?"

"No, I'm going. It's almost six, so Ryuuji needs to make dinner, right?"

It was exactly as Taiga said. The breadwinner of the house, who needed dinner by seven no matter how much mental damage he had taken, was waiting for him. Ryuuji also slowly got up and handed the coffee money over to Taiga, who held some bills. Taiga also received change from Ami and went to pay the check by herself.

Ami went around the table, and Ryuuji tried to follow after her.

"Whoa?!"

Suddenly, Ami grabbed his collar. Although she was a girl, her power was tyrannical, and he reflexively tried to shake her off.

"It would have been better if you were the only one who really got hurt," she said.

"What?! What are you talking about?!"

Behind her sunglasses, Ami opened her eyes wider than he had ever seen her do before. He realized she was glaring at him.

"You're an idiot, so you wouldn't get it anyway."

Her lips were contorted as though she were smiling, but she was probably incredibly annoyed.

"I really do hate you."

"..."

He stumbled as she pushed him away. Ami turned on her heel, and she simply said, "I'm out first." With an elegant catwalk, she left the café.

If you were the only one who really got hurt.

Ami seemed exactly like she had on the night of the party. She'd gotten angry and left him in the same way.

The origin of her irritation was probably what she'd said back when they were preparing for the party. Ami had teased him for having a father-daughter-like relationship with Taiga. Minori was playing at being the mom, she'd said. She'd said they should stop doing that if they didn't want to get really hurt...but she'd also said to forget she ever said anything.

He couldn't forget it though—and right now, he really had been incredibly hurt after Minori rejected him. Did that really happen because he and Taiga pulled Minori into a pseudo-family situation, just as Ami said?

If it wasn't just him, then who else was hurt?

"You always leave out something!"

If she was going to insult him for being an idiot, then why couldn't she have explained it in a way an idiot like him could understand? Ryuuji muttered to himself. If she really was more grown up than everyone else, and knew what was going on around her better than anyone, then she should have told him what was going on, too. She just understood for herself, got angry for herself, and left him in the dust. It was selfish.

That's how you always are.

"Did Dimhuahua go home? What's wrong with you? It's like you've been shot in your Achilles heel and murdered," said Taiga, who had finished paying the check and was looking questioningly up at Ryuuji. He was standing stock-still. His face was frozen.

◆✳◆

They left Pseudobucks. When they started walking, the sky was completely dark. The night was cold, and the northern wind nearly made them stop breathing.

"You haven't gone shopping yet, right? Shouldn't you hurry up?"

"What about you?"

"I'm headed to the station. They made a new bento box place near the ticket gates."

They separated on the shopping street. Along the national highway, the T-shaped, desolate road stank of car exhaust. The road was closed off to pedestrians at that point.

"It's cold!" Taiga said, scowling under the streetlights.

The light from the bridge that went over the river could be seen straight ahead, but it was still a ways off. To the left of the T intersection was the station, and to the right was the supermarket. Basically, he would be separating from Taiga there until they met at school the next day. They wouldn't have a chance to talk between now and then. Though he was a little hesitant, there was something Ryuuji thought he needed to tell her.

"So when you were talking about the opportunity to check what Minori's real feelings are, what you meant was the school trip."

"That's right. You completely forgot about it, didn't you?"

"I did. Putting aside whether Ami clings to me or not...I didn't think that you thought about things that much. So, thanks for that. But I think you've gone out of your way to say some stuff you didn't need to. You didn't really have to tell her that."

Taiga buttoned the front of her coat and shook her head.

"It's better just to tell it to Dimhuahua straight. And I feel like I'm to blame for this. I said so already, right? That night, I forced things. I think the results would definitely have been different otherwise."

Her mouth contorted slightly as she slowly looked up to the heavens, as though she were searching for stars in the pale night sky.

"About Christmas Eve, what do you think Minorin said to me?"

It was as though she were saying it to herself. Taiga turned her gaze to Ryuuji.

"She said, 'There wasn't anything anyway.' She said that you were just trying to cheer her up while she was down and that you were kind, and there wasn't anything else to it. That's what she said. She kept saying it was nothing, it was nothing, it was nothing. And then she smiled, that girl."

"Maybe she really didn't think there was anything there?"

"You idiot."

Under the streetlight, Taiga stopped looking for the stars and turned her face to Ryuuji. With her delicate fingers, she held back her hair, which was floating in the wind, and told him, "You and Minorin really do have reciprocated feelings. It really should work out. Like actually."

Seeing Taiga's resolute and complete self-confidence as she asserted that, Ryuuji finally wanted to ask her. Right then, it was kind of like he was in a frame of mind where he couldn't just let her words go.

"I've been wanting to ask you...where did you get the idea that Minori likes me? You can't say you just know from looking."

"You want to know?"

Taiga tilted her head under the streetlight. She smiled a little, as though she were a magician introducing a trick or like a witch actually showing him real magic. Full of confidence, she opened her arms up to Ryuuji and looked grandly at him.

"Then, you have to make a promise. You can't say anything stupid like 'Huh?' or 'There's no way' or 'That's unbelievable.' If you vow that, I'll tell you."

"I won't say that stuff. I won't. I vow it."

He raised one hand and took an oath. Ryuuji waited for Taiga's magic. Taiga nodded haughtily.

"Then I'll tell you. The reason I believe in that is in me."

That's what she said.

That was it.

Disappointed, Ryuuji was about to ask her, *Huh?* Then he remembered the oath and shut his mouth.

"Basically, I believe in *you*. I think that you're the right person for Minorin to love. Your only motive is to love her."

Taiga smiled as though making it all out to be a joke. Then she simply turned on her heel.

"Bye! See you tomorrow!"

She started running down the street towards the station, all on her own. In the middle, she turned around, as though remembering something. She made a grimace and raised her voice.

"Come to think of it, your attitude today was the worst! What was with that?! Tomorrow, you can't run away! You don't actually want to run, right?!"

Taiga didn't wait for Ryuuji's reply but once again turned her back to him. This time, she didn't look back as she ran. Her back was small, like a child's, and he immediately lost sight of her.

Left behind, Ryuuji held his chest. His heart was thumping. It really did seem like magic. That was what his heart told him.

His heart, which had suffered so much, regained its warm pulse just from what Taiga had said. If Taiga said that—if she said that she would believe in him—then he would believe all he needed was for Taiga to believe.

With that small act of magic, his courage returned, and Ryuuji also started walking the night alone. That was when a thought occurred to him.

If Ami had seen him thinking so simply, she definitely would have fixed him with her freezing gaze and said, "You really don't understand anything."

What a terrible thought.

"GOOOOOD MORNING!"

When his voice cracked grossly, Minori immediately turned around.

In the cold of midwinter, a group of fluffed-up sparrows moved from inside the azalea bush next to them to Ryuuji and Minori's feet. He didn't know what they were so passionately pecking at, but they all started hammering away rapidly at the asphalt.

"Yo! Yo! Ma!"

Startled by Minori's buoyant voice, they all scattered into the air.

The weather was clear, and the sun came at them blindingly on that below-freezing morning. The beams of light made Minori's round cheeks light up as she struck a salute.

Ryuuji squinted his eyes and looked back at her, though he felt like lowering his head. He wanted to turn his eyes down, but

he desperately raised them up. He tried very hard to move his fal-
tering mouth. If he ran away now, it'd end up being like yesterday.

"So a-about yesterday...uh, sorry. Uh, um...it ended up seem-
ing like I was ignoring you."

Minori waited for him to finish his awkward apology.

"Whatchu talkin' about, Takasu-kun? Seriously, just stop that!"

She gave him a good look at her white teeth as she smiled.
As her face wrinkled from the grin, she looked like a radiant sun-
flower that had bloomed in the middle of winter. She rewrapped
her tartan-checked scarf, pushed up her slightly shorter bangs,
and shifted up the heavy-looking sports bag on her shoulder.

"I just thought you had a stomachache or something!"

She seemed to leap forward as she approached him by a step.
She probably didn't actually think that, but understood the awkwardness that caused Ryuuji to run. "So, doesn't matta' to me at all!"

Even so, Minori smiled, and Ryuuji smiled for her, too. For
the first time in what seemed like forever, they faced each other.
They were exactly a meter apart.

"It did ache a little...actually."

"Wow, what a shocking confession."

His smile wasn't manufactured. There were no lies or tricks
or deceptions.

He smiled so he could ride through it, so that after being
rejected, he could head forward. Ride this out and smile, let the
storm finish, and wait for the next scene. He had seen it on TV
once. Supposedly when kids and adults were involved in the same

accident, the kids would sometimes make it through with unexpectedly fewer injuries than the adults. They could do that because their bodies were still flexible. They would be sent flying and hit the hard ground, but survive with minimal damage to their bodies. Their flexibility alone would act as a cushion to protect their lives.

Using the same logic, he would smile and smile as much as he needed and flexibly take it in, he thought. He would be as pliable as he could. If he took everything seriously, he really would be pulverized.

Smile, Takasu Ryuuji. Smile, Kushieda Minori, he commanded, but that didn't seem to actually translate onto his face. Minori seemed taken aback.

"Whoa!"

It was fine as long as the kids were smiling.

He recalled Taiga's face from long ago. *I ain't dead yet...* the vision of Tiger said as she put a doughnut ring over her head and smiled.

As for the real Taiga...

"Minoriiiin! Good morning!"

She completely ignored Ryuuji's existence, waving her hand from the other side of the crosswalk, where the light was red. "Yooo yooo!" Minori waved both of her hands back.

Taiga awkwardly waved around both her arms and her legs. "Yooo yooo yooo!" The young salaryman also waiting for the light behind Taiga seemed appalled as he watched her wiggling dance in silence.

What an embarrassment, Ryuuji thought.

"Yooo yooo yooo! Yooooo!" For some reason, Minori became even more enthusiastic. "Yo yo yo! Good morning yo! Good mor-yo-ning! Good-yo mor-yo-ning yo! Ahh!"

She swung around the bag on her shoulder and vigorously mimed a DJ move. Minori held a headphone only she could feel with one hand and a record only she could see with the other. She scratched it and made it squeal. Facing the floor only she could perceive, she raised her voice to a falsetto to rile up the crowd. "Haaah! Aaah!"

"Minorin, what do you think you're doing?! That's weird!"

Taiga laughed from the opposite side of the road. The unsettled salaryman at her back stared at Minori this time. Then, the man noticed that next to the crazy Minori was Ryuuji, with a face that looked like a depiction of the demon Asura that a cursed sculptor had carved with a bloodstained chisel. Slowly, the man's eyes turned away.

It wasn't that Ryuuji was thinking, "If you look at my girl Kushieda like that then, why, I'll—I'll—I'll kill ya!" He was just genuinely taken aback by DJ Minori.

"Give it a rest, Kushieda... You're embarrassing other people. I'm going to go ahead of you."

"Whyyy? I'll go with you."

"No. It's hard to keep up with you and Taiga."

He had dispelled the awkwardness of the other day. That was enough for now. Ryuuji started to hurriedly walk ahead.

"Ohh! Minorin, Ryuuji's running! Grab him!" Taiga wailed from the other side of the light.

It wasn't just Ryuuji who didn't understand what Taiga was getting at. "Huh?! I need to grab him?!" Minori questioned back.

"Yeah!" Taiga replied.

Ryuuji's eyes met with Minori's when she turned around, and he reflexively whipped the other way. Minori was also acting on reflex as she reached out a hand to him before he could escape. His cold hand and hers hit each other. Minori's fingers latched on to Ryuuji's.

"Ack!"

She held his fingers for barely a fleeting second.

Naturally, Ryuuji leapt up. He was so surprised, he couldn't even yell. He felt like he had been struck by a bolt of lightning that worked itself from his fingertips all the way down to his tailbone. However, Minori was the one who let go first.

Ahh! She might have even said. Or it might have been, *Gyaa!*

Minori's fingers went limp. She pulled her hand to her chest as though she had been burned and enveloped it in her other hand. Her face was red. It was as though Ryuuji had done something wrong to her or she was scared. Her mouth was set in a line. She leered at him.

"Ahh, damn it, don't underestimate me!" she barked. She reached out her hand again for a second try.

"Deeeetaaaaaaiiiiiiiinnnnn!" she yelled self-importantly, but all she grabbed was the cuff of his school jacket...and only the very edge of it to boot. He would have been able to shake her off just by lifting his arm, but Ryuuji simply let himself be detained. Actually, to be more accurate, he was just so shocked that he couldn't move.

At that point, the light turned green. Taiga looked right and left and right again one more time before she started running. She looked at Ryuuji as Minori held him by the sleeve, and then she looked at Minori. After that, she smiled.

"You got caught, so you get to hold the bags!"

"Whoa?!"

She threw her bag at Ryuuji. The bag traced a parabola, and Ryuuji caught it without thinking about it. Taiga pointed at Ryuuji and danced slightly. "Hah!" Having lightened her load, she spread her arms out to the sides like an airplane.

"He fell for it! He fell for it! I'm heading out first!"

Her skirt billowed as she ran away.

"You're going first... Wait, Taiga, you've got to be kidding me! What?! What am I supposed to do with this?! You're seriously making me carry it?!"

The bag Taiga had left in his hand wasn't really that heavy, but he was bitter. First she teased him for being a dog and a bug, and now she made him her bag carrier—even if she did it so he could walk to school with Minori, couldn't she have accomplished that some other way?

He watched her disappear into the distance in mute amazement.

"This is your fault, Kushieda. Why did you have to catch me?"

Ryuuji looked at Minori. Minori, in her own way, was dumbfounded where she stood.

"That Taiga...Taiga...Taiga..." she repeated like a prayer. Suddenly, she shook herself like a wet dog, and her eyes went wide. She swung her arm around coolly, like a hero that was about to change into their costume. Then she brought her fist up to her chest. "No...this isn't a big deal. Now! Give me a cord!"

"A cord?" said Ryuuji.

"I mean one of these!"

She took one of the two handles of the bag that Ryuuji was holding. The bag hung between them, almost as though they were small kids holding a shopping bag.

"All right. Seriously, Taiga's just hopeless. I'll finish her off when we get to school."

She grinned up at him from a close distance. Her cheek had the texture of a peach, and the smell of her hair... Ryuuji froze now, of all times.

"Right!"

"Uh...yeah!"

They swiftly decided to finish off Taiga right then and there.

As they walked, Minori said, "Oh, time out." She pulled out gloves from her pocket and put them on her hands. Still not saying anything, she rubbed her hands together. "Okay!" She once again took up half the bag.

Now that he was suddenly alone with her, he couldn't escape anymore. It really wouldn't have been appropriate for him to run now. He wouldn't do that. As Ryuuji walked, he attempted to strike up a natural conversation. Like an idiot, he tried to calculate the right time to talk. "Ah, I, uh..."

"Hm? You trying to get me in my pressure point?"

"No. I...I just think your hair looks pretty neat."

He'd finally said it.

"Oh, *si*. I wanted to make it shorter, but the beautician said that I've got a large crown, and I shouldn't go short. She said my hair is stiff, so it'd probably stick out and make my head look super big. She kind of scared me out of it."

She kept facing forward. As she breathed out white, Minori's voice lowered as though she were a little disappointed. "I wanted to get a pixie cut, though. I wanted it to actually be kind of like... like a man's! I wanted it to have a force behind it. Like a boy cut! Like a bowl cut! ...No that's not right... Like an undercut! That's wrong, too..."

"Well, maybe it would have looked good short?"

Minori raised her face and looked at Ryuuji. She smiled and said, "Yeah, you're right." She used one knit-gloved hand to lightly push up her hair several times. "When I was in elementary school, I pretty much had a buzz cut. I went with my little brother to this place called The Barber. They really only cut hair for men, but he'd just shear everything off with the clippers. My nickname used to be Mister Lady."

"Really...well that's... Mister Lady... Wait, you've got a brother? He's a high school baseball player, right?"

"Yeah. He's one year younger. Their school is pretty good, and they go to the Koshien Stadium championships pretty often. Of course, he's not one of the main players, but next year he might pitch at the Koshien mound. I can't believe that jerk's a pitcher."

"Wow, I had no idea. That's pretty amazing. You must be proud of him."

"Well, I'm super jealous of him. Ahhh, when we were in little league, I was way ahead of him. Now I'm just like a lamb chop that can't even get a shear."

"I think you'll be fine without that. Actually, you mean a lamb, not a lamb chop, right?"

"Oh, Takasu-kun, you said such a shockingly lame thing that I've got static in my hair."

"It's because you're playing with your hair with gloves," he said back as he side-eyed Minori. Her hair was standing on end. He saw her neck peek from under her scarf and thought, *It really would have been fine short.*

That was when he noticed it. At some point, he'd become able to smile without making a conscious effort. He could walk next to Minori while holding the bag with her. He had gathered up the pieces of his shattered heart and squeezed them together, like making a rice ball. He wouldn't run. He would hold his ground.

He was sure he could keep going like this. It was almost as though nothing had happened. It was like he could start afresh.

Right. The upcoming school trip was another chance. That was when he would slowly come to face her.

If he did that during the trip, just as Taiga had told him, there was a chance he could get a different answer from Minori.

Ryuuji believed it. The time was right to have courage and face forward.

"Okay, let's finish off Taiga! Where'd she go?!"

"She's not here. How about the bathroom? The lockers?"

"We'll find her even if we have to turn over every blade of grass! This is punishment! It's Hamburger Hill!"

No sooner had they gotten to the classroom than Minori had started to huff and puff as she began looking around for Taiga. Though he was a little exasperated, Ryuuji was with her after having agreed to it earlier.

At that point, he locked eyes with Ami, who it seemed had arrived at school earlier. Ami was chit-chatting with Maya, Nanako, and the other girls who surrounded her. Seeing Minori arrive with Ryuuji, she turned toward them with slightly narrowed eyes. However, before he could understand her expression, Minori also noticed Ami.

"Oh! Ahmin-senpai! It's the first time I've seen you this year! Have you seen that girl Taiga?"

"Oh my, good morning, Minori-chan. I haven't seen Tiger but...well, how do I put this, it's like, *ugh*."

Right, Takasu-kun, she kept going.

He wondered what would happen if he walked right over there and just gave her a double slap. *What're you trying to say?!*

He wouldn't do it, but he wanted to. What in the world was she suddenly trying to start?

"Ugh?"

He didn't know what she was trying to say, but he knew the words aimed directly at Minori were meant to be prickly, and they had left Minori standing stock-still. He wasn't sure he knew what was going on, so he ended up just standing stock-still, too.

"Well, I wonder what it could mean. What could it be?"

Like a ripple, something stirred delicately between Ami and Minori. At that time, Taiga, who had no idea what was going on, came into the classroom through the hallway.

"Oh! Found Taiga!"

That ripple was drowned in their normal, everyday life.

They had their long homeroom that afternoon.

Leaving the class to Kitamura, the bachelorette (age 30) was reading some thick magazine... If you looked really, really closely, it was a free housing information magazine you could get at the station. She was completely in her own world. The groups in the class were also in leisure mode and filling up on their lunches. There were even a few of them already dozing off.

"Now, we're going to start the long homeroom. Stop messing around and open your eyes, everyone." Kitamura started talking from the teacher's platform, but he also seemed relaxed somehow, and there wasn't any power behind his words.

"Today's the day we're going to decide on groups for the school trip you've all been waiting for."

We haven't been waiting for it, someone heckled. Kitamura, who probably wasn't waiting for the trip either anyway, didn't say anything back.

"We're making eight-person groups with four girls and four boys each."

He started writing on the blackboard in squiggling script. The *4, 4, 8* he wrote was slanted and distorted.

In the lax classroom, Ryuuji was the only one with a grim expression, his spine ramrod-straight. He felt like a swordsman, but he looked like a delinquent. He was trying to be enthusiastic, but he was worried about the atmosphere of the class.

To Ryuuji, the school trip was an incredibly important affair. There wouldn't be any other opportunities to revive his relationship with Minori after this. But the class seemed lifeless, like they hated the idea. A few of them even whispered here and there that they would rather have the class trip canceled. Naturally, no one seemed to want to go to a snowy mountain in the middle of the winter.

"Okay, let's start making the groups. During this time, we'll make a list of names to present."

At Kitamura's lackadaisical order, some of the students started to stand up and walk around as they exchanged dull conversation.

"Ah well, this is so lame."

"Ugh, let's pair up."

"Hey, Takasu. We're teaming up, right? Also that idiot and—"

Noto trotted (uncutely) over to Ryuuji's seat. Then he pointed at Haruta, who was sleeping out of disappointment that the Okinawa trip had been canceled. His eyes had rolled up into his head to the point that they could see the whites.

"Plus the master!" Noto pointed.

"Add me in, too," Kitamura was saying as he waved his hand gracefully like a politician in an election from the teacher's platform.

"Now we've got four—boy team complete!"

As Ryuuji looked at the happy-looking otter's face, he felt a little like he had been saved. They wouldn't have the added flair of the sky, sea, and sightseeing anymore for the school trip, but if he were with his friends, he would be having more than enough fun. If he wanted to make the trip fruitful, then he would need to take the lead. He would need to show them he was having fun and make his friends excited, too.

He cocked his chin up. He'd put them out of their misery... no, he meant he'd end their misery. Ryuuji's eyes glinted as he opened them wide—he wasn't mimicking the face of a raptor going after an otter, though.

"Right! All we've got left is the girl team."

He wasn't mimicking a pervert ogling the girl team, either. He wanted to be in the same group as Minori. That was all he desired. However, in a move completely unrelated to Ryuuji's motives, Noto prodded at Ryuuji's elbow and laughed uncutely. "Nah ha ha ha!"

"Let's pair up with Tiger's group! We'll put Kitamura and Tiger in the same group, right?!"

"You're still trying to do that..."

"We're going on such a plain ski trip. Don't you want to add a little spice with some love?"

Ryuuji sighed. His enthusiasm disappeared into the air with the carbon dioxide he exhaled. Even though he wanted everyone to be excited, he was already getting tired of Noto playing matchmaker half in jest to get Kitamura and Taiga together.

Of course, he wanted Taiga and Kitamura in the same group. If that happened, Taiga would also be happy. But...how should he put this? He felt like it was so unnecessary having people who weren't even involved trying to make a big deal about deliberately manufacturing ways to get them together. If Taiga needed any help, then she only needed it from Ryuuji. Someone like Noto would never understand Taiga's complex, weird personality and behavior patterns, anyway.

Ryuuji tried to say, "You rubbernecker!" or "Get your neck out of other people's business!" but got distracted. A little ways away, two girls clung to each other. Their faces were smooshed together.

"It's such a boring trip, but if you're there with me, I'm sure it'll be fun!"

"Yeah, I feel exactly the same, Minoriiiin!"

Minori and Taiga were passionately talking to each other. They were completely joined at the hip. In other words, if he were in the same group as Taiga, then he would automatically be in the same group as Minori. He didn't know how he hadn't realized such a simple thing. If he just entrusted himself to Noto's scheme, then everything would come right together.

Regardless...

"You rubbernecker! Get your neck out of other people's business!"

"What?! But don't you think it'd be fun? It'd be super funny for sure if Tiger and Kitamura ended up dating. Kitamura's probably on the verge of forgetting the patriarch at any second, and Tiger's in love with Kitamura, so it'd be like she's finally getting her chance!"

"I'm saying you shouldn't butt in!"

"Takasu, you're so... Well, it doesn't matter. Actually, Tiger and Kushieda haven't got any other girls with them, right? What are we going to do for the other two? I wonder if Ami-chan would join us? That'd be amazing."

You mean that girl who started off the morning spouting gibberish and then ignored me the rest of the day since she hates me because I'm an idiot? You mean that Ami-chan? Ryuuji casually looked around the classroom and found Ami, who was forming one part of the usual it-girl trifecta. For some reason, Maya was getting worked up, saying, "Yeah, why not, let's invite them!"

Ami faltered, "What? Seriously?" Nanako was looking at the two in amusement. Around the three of them, groups of boys were holding themselves in check and just speechlessly watching. All the boys were putting off an I-want-them-to-be-in-our-group aura.

Nope, not gonna happen. Ryuuji shook his head at Noto.

"No way," he said. "Kawashima and Taiga actually hate each other's guts, and even if they didn't, she's always in a group of three with Kihara and Kashii anyway. We'd be off by one."

"Oh, you're right. But it would have been a great plan with Kitamura and Tiger and me and Ami-chan."

"Pull your head out of your butt and stop spouting the impossible."

"What? In my imagination, I can spread my wings and be free in the skies as I fly! Hey, Kushieda 'n' Tiger! Would you join us?!"

Getting carried away, he waved his hand as he headed over to them. Minori and Taiga glared at him in jest.

"What do you wanna do, Taiga? Looks like some men are heading over to see if they can join our ranks."

"How about we slash him shoulder to hip, Minorin?"

Translated loosely, that was probably a yes.

Taiga casually looked over at Ryuuji, took a glance at Minori, and once again returned her gaze to him. It was as though she were saying, *Look at you, getting into the same group as Minorin.* Ryuuji returned the look—well, he didn't exactly, but he did try to indicate, *You got in the same group with Kitamura, too.* He was about to try pointing casually at Kitamura on the teacher's platform.

"Hey, Maruo! Will you join our group?!"

Oh no. His eyes peeled open.

He had been careless, and Maya had found her opening to happily slip over to Kitamura on the teacher's platform. Kitamura, being Kitamura, didn't know they were joining Taiga's group.

"Yeah, sure," he readily nodded. At this rate, they'd end up double-booked.

"Huh?! Wait, wait, master, what do you think you're doing!"

Noto headed over to the teacher's platform in a fluster, cutting between Kitamura and Maya with ragged karate chops.

"Nuh-uh, nope, not gonna happen! Get away from each other! Break it up! Sorry Kihara, but Master Kitamura is in our group, and we already promised to join Tiger's group!"

"What?! Seriously?!"

Actually, who said we needed you?! Clear to the point it was scary, those words seemed to be written on Maya's face as she looked at Noto. As far as Maya was concerned, Ryuuji, Haruta, and every non-Kitamura person in the group was probably unnecessary.

Noto pushily put his arm around Kitamura's shoulders. "Let's go, let's make the group listings and write out our names." He quickly tried to lead Kitamura away. Maya reached out an agitated hand.

"You've got Maruo-kun, Noto-kun, Takasu-kun and Haruta-kun in your group, right?"

Nanako, who had been watching the situation together with Ami from a distance, approached them. When her calm voice intercepted them, it seemed to have power behind it, and Noto stopped walking without thinking.

"Then in that case, I think you have to ask the other members what their opinions are. Hey, Haruta-kun, wake up. Wake...up!"

As though she were breathing life back into him, Nanako spoke sweetly to Haruta in his unconscious state. He was like a corpse as he slept. He was the seventeen-year-old Sir Sleeps-a-lot. He wouldn't wake up if an elephant stepped on him. And yet, Haruta's white eyes slowly regained their consciousness.

"Hey, Haruta-kun... Who do you like better, us or those girls?"

"Huah...?"

Haruta's eyes first went to Nanako and Ami, then to Maya. Next, he looked at Taiga and Minori, whom Nanako was pointing to.

"Uhhhn...you..."

He started to walk unsteadily as though drawn to Nanako.

"Well, thanks. You can go back to sleep now...forever... permanently..."

Nanako rotated her finger in circles in front of Haruta's eyes. Haruta stared intently at her finger and his eyes moved over and over in a circle. Then he simply collapsed right onto the floor.

Ami said in a small voice, "You're amazing, Nanako."

Maya applauded. "That was super spiritual."

"Haruta's brain is on the level of a dragonfly's..."

Is our friend a dragonfly? Is he? Noto whispered in sadness. Ryuuji dodged the question as he tried to wake up the pitiful Haruta.

Maya glared at Noto, as though saying, *Now what'll you do?* Noto narrowed his eyes at Maya while Kitamura stayed sandwiched between them. Taiga and Minori seemed unable to follow the developments and were looking at each other in worry. Kitamura seemed even more worried. He realized that the situation had come about because of his carefree response and rubbed at the bridge of his nose where his glasses rested.

Ryuuji understood that Maya wanted to be paired with her beloved Maruo, aka Kitamura, but did Ami want that? He glanced sneakily at Ami to see what she was doing. If she partnered with Kitamura, she would need to be in the same group as Ryuuji—the one she claimed to hate because he was stupid. Maybe she really did intend to skip out? Maybe she wouldn't go on the once-in-a-lifetime school trip?

Ami, who might not have noticed Ryuuji's gaze or who might just be ignoring it, was only looking at Maya.

"Huh?! Wait a second, isn't this just perfect?!"

At that point, the ever-popular Kitamura realized an important fact and raised his voice.

"Kihara and you guys make up a group of three, right? And Kushieda and Taiga make two. We have sixteen boys and seventeen girls in our class, so one group needs to have four boys and five girls. Isn't that a relief? We figured it all out!"

Whaaat?! The one who raised her voice to the ceiling was Maya. She'd attained her goal of being in the same group as Kitamura, but her wide, apricot-shaped eyes were confused as they looked at Taiga. In Maya's imagination, now that the patriarch was out of the picture, the last boss to defeat in her battle for Kitamura was Aisaka Taiga.

On the other side of things, Taiga wasn't even looking at Kitamura, even though they were in the same group.

"Huuh?! I have to be with *you*?!" Ami exclaimed. "I don't want to though! Oh, right, we could just have only Minori join our group! Then you could be a lone Tiger and just wander around by yourself!"

"How about you go around looking for your own tribe, Dimhuahua? Oh, look, look, I think there's someone right there you'd get along with."

"Why are you lumping me together with the spinster (age 30)?!"

Taiga and Ami, busy sparring verbally, didn't notice Maya's complicated gaze. Eventually Maya quietly approached Ryuuji, who she must have decided was an ally.

"This'll be a struggle for both of us, right? But we have to keep at it! Actually, that Noto! That Noto guy...! He's sooo infuriating!"

As though trying to get his sympathy, she opened her eyes wide at him.

"Um, you must be misunderstanding something. It's not really like Taiga is my cru—"

He tried to tell it to her straight, but Maya already stopped listening. "Maruo! Let's write the list out together!" She followed after Kitamura, running at him like a bullet.

Ryuuji breathed out a sigh as he watched her and then somehow mustered his composure.

"You're having a fight again?! Let's be nice, Ahmin!"

"Oh, of course I'm fine with you, Minori-chan. ♥ Taiga's the one who's a nuisance!"

"Your partner, Dimhuahua, is writing in red pen in a real estate magazine. Why don't you go help her out?"

"Like I said, why is my partner the spinster (age 30)?!"

They were making a ruckus like usual. Taiga, Ami, and then Minori's voices were soaring into his ears. *Everything's like normal.* As he realized he didn't see any changes in Ami and Minori's relationship, Ryuuji breathed a sigh of relief.

Hee hee hee.

"...?"

He had a dream where all the girls were laughing.

In the lingering laughter, Ryuuji slowly opened his heavy eyes from where he was curled up under the covers. He looked at his clock to check the time and was struck with horror for a moment.

It was nine in the morning, but it was Sunday, so he could sleep in. He had plans, but they weren't meeting up until way later.

He closed his eyes again and tried to bury himself back into the covers.

"He definitely hasn't noticed yet, right?"

"Yeah, he's going back to sleep."

His eyes opened with such force they might have torn apart. It wasn't that his memories of being a demon lord in another life had awakened within him—he'd just heard some people talking nearby.

The curtains were left open a good fifteen centimeters, and through that gap, instead of the morning light, he had a perfect view of the window of Taiga's condo. He saw two faces there.

"Whoa?!"

"Oh, he's awake!"

"Oh no! He saw us!"

He got up, opened the curtains to check what was going on in the reality outside his dreams, and almost collapsed. He somehow righted himself and promptly closed the curtains.

Just now what what what what what...whoa! It only took a moment for him to be clearly awakened to the fact that what had just happened wasn't a dream, but reality.

"Ryuuji! You can't escape from reality! Get up!"

"Hey, Taiga. He looks sleepy. That's kind of harsh."

Taiga and Minori had been peeping at him while he slept. On this day, of all days, he was a mess—he was wearing the most linty, pilled set of pajamas he owned. Plus, with the worst timing...

"Oh dear...I just heard Taiga-chan's voice..."

Normally dead asleep, his mother Yasuko came out of the bathroom. Staggering like a zombie, she headed unsteadily into her son's room. He tried to keep her at bay, but she got on the bed and flung open the curtains he had only just closed, so everything was exposed.

"Ohh. ★ It really is Taiga-chan. ★ Oh, nice to meet your friend. ★"

She waved her hand in a carefree manner at the peeping couple.

"Ya-chan, good morning! Minorin, that's Ryuuji's mom."

"Good morning to you! Oh dear! I'm Kushieda! Oh dear! Sorry for doing something so unreasonable, Ms. Takasu! Oh dear! To Bomba! Oh dear! To Bomba! Oh—"

"Minorin, you'll burst a vessel in your head."

It was true that on that morning, Yasuko had a bomba hair style that could only be described as something a country bumpkin would have. She hadn't washed out her half-updo, which she had hardened like a rock with hairspray, before bed. It always ended up like that when she didn't. At least she had washed off her makeup. Yasuko smiled, her soft cheeks bouncing like mochi. She sniffled.

"Naugh, Ryuu-chaaan, I'm cowld."

"It's 'cause you opened the windows up all the way! Put something on...wait, eek...noooo!"

Even her son was taken aback at the way she looked. She was in a barely-there bra and pilled wool underwear. *Oh no, this won't do. It'll look exactly like we're a family of perverts.* Ryuuji panicked and closed the curtains. *Fsssshht!*

"Oh, right! Let's all eat breakfast together. ★ Ryuu-chan will make it."

Fshhht! Yasuko pushed aside her son and opened the curtains, still in only her bra.

"We can't, Ya-chan. Actually, we already made breakfast, and we're eating it after this."

"Oh, you did? But I'm so lonely..."

Taiga, leaning her elbows on the windowsill next to Minori, giggled.

"We got together early, and we're spending our morning together, right, Minorin?"

"Yay! That's how it is, so we'll see you later, Takasu-kun."

Right—the school trip group had promised to meet at Taiga's house at lunch. They needed to make a guidebook for school and couldn't meet at the family restaurant because they needed to use a computer. In a rare moment for her, Taiga had offered up her house. It seemed Minori had also come to the condo by herself early in the morning.

Ryuuji casually hid Yasuko with his shoulders and also hid his own pilled pajamas with the curtain as he looked at Taiga.

"You're going to have Kushieda help clean your place, aren't you? You probably haven't even done any spring cleaning. It's definitely dirty...hmph!"

It probably sounded like he held a grudge, and that was correct. Ryuuji had told her several times that he'd come over to help with spring cleaning, but for some reason or other, Taiga kept making excuses to reject him. It was enough to make his face go Devilman.

"Whomp whomp. You're wrong. My whole condo is sparkling clean from floor to ceiling. It might even be cleaner than your place. Right, Minorin, isn't it clean?"

Yeah, yeah! Minori nodded.

"That's a lie! There's no way! You don't have anyone to clean..."

"I do. The Duskin Merry Maids did it. Ahh, it was such an ordeal. Yesterday, four old maids came in and took three hours scrubbing here and there and who-knows-where..."

"Wha...at?!"

Did she mean those thorough Merry Maids who cost at least thirty thousand yen? Did she mean to say that those pros had cleaned the bottom of the laundry machine, the curtain rails, the air conditioner filter, and everything Ryuuji had been eyeing for so long?

"The skills of a real pro are definitely on another level. Well, Ryuuji, you can just take your time coming in later. Minorin and I are going to relish our breakfast, and then we're going to the Uniqlo at the station building at ten and buying Heattech tank tops and tights to bring on the school trip... In other words, it's girl time, and you'd better not come."

"Oh, Taiga, it just dinged. Looks like the bread is toasted."

"Really?! We need to eat it while it's still hot! Bye, Ryuuji!"

The two of them pitter-pattered away from the window and disappeared. At some point, Yasuko had flopped over on her son's bed and was back asleep in a position that was painful to look at.

Ryuuji's fingers trembled where they were on the window frame.

She's hired the Duskin...Merry Maids? He looked at the Takasu stick that he used to clean the window frame. The Merry Maids probably had such amazing cleaning supplies. They probably used electricity to their heart's content and scrubbed at Taiga's condo with mechanical appliances. Those maids had stepped into Ryuuji's domain using money-wasting techniques on all the things he had been letting develop for spring cleaning.

Those Merry Maids... Those damn Merry Maids! Ryuuji chewed bitterly on his lip and rubbed at the window frame with his pilled pajama sleeve. Yasuko had left fingerprints on it!

At the movement of her son jiggling around, Yasuko fell right off the mattress.

Whoa. The word seemed to float above the group sitting around the low glass table.

"I'm going to bring the computer and printer from my bedroom, so wait here. Minorin, could you help me carry the cables and power supply?"

"Okay."

Taiga took along Minori and left the living room. No sooner had she done that than everyone burst out talking.

"Wait, wait, wait a second! Isn't this room amazing?! It's basically the same size as my place!"

"This must be a condo, right? The furniture is super cute, too...

She said she lived alone, but maybe she's like super rich? I'd become her roommate anytime if she wanted."

"Me too! Me too! Me too!"

Maya was there in a turtleneck, miniskirt, and leggings. Whether it was a coincidence or not, Nanako subtly matched her with a turtleneck, dress, and leggings. Ryuuji passed around floor cushions to each of them and, at the sight of the excited girls, nostalgically remembered his own reaction to the condo.

Kyaah, what an amazing condo, how luxurious... When he stepped into it on that first morning, Ryuuji had been enchanted as he looked around the room. And then—"Ugh!" He had stopped in his tracks, close to throwing up at the rotting smell coming from the kitchen. *This is terrible. I need to do something.* And so, he had started cleaning—in other words, that was definitely when his and Taiga's destinies had first intersected. If that smell did him in and he ran home, where would they be now?

"It's like something that'd be in a magazine... Actually, Takasu-kun, could you stop wiping everything we touch?"

"Oh, sorry. It's a bad habit..."

He had unconsciously been wiping up the glass the girls touched with the towel he had in hand. No matter whether they were the Merry Maids or not, they couldn't do this full-detail support cleaning.

"Whoa! That's a huge TV!"

"The lights are huge, too!"

They gasped at the TV and gawked at the chandelier. Noto and Kitamura, who were taken aback by every little thing, looked like they were having fun, too. Then Kitamura turned to Ryuuji.

"I'd heard about it before, but you were serious about Aisaka's house being right next to yours."

"Huh, next to yours?! Takasu-kun, do you live in this condo, too?! Amazing!"

At Maya's overexaggerated voice, he shook his head. *No, no, no, no, no, that'll never happen!*

"My house is the rental next door. The windows face each other exactly. Well, that's the thing that connected me and Taiga together and made us close... I guess not close, but it made us get to know each other...like normal in the classroom."

"Guess you two are inseparable, whether you like it or not."

Noto's words were probably right, in the end, so Ryuuji nodded.

Ami sat next to Maya in her skinny jeans, her long legs folded and sprawled out in boredom. The pale skin above the cleavage of her knitted top was adorned by a delicate gold chain necklace.

Making a guidebook was a boring and simple task. Ami, who normally would never participate in something like that, had been threatened by Taiga into coming.

"If you're thinking of skipping the menial work," she said, "then we might have a DVD appreciation day at my house. Are you okay with that?"

It was likely the DVDs Taiga meant were the ones he only heard about in rumor, which starred Kawashima Ami and were produced at the command of Aisaka Taiga. It was titled "One Hundred Impressions in Quick Succession."

"Hey, isn't this amazing?! Anyone could look cute if they wore this princess-y thing!"

Haruta, whom Ryuuji could no longer see at that point, had appeared in a ridiculous getup. At some point, he had gotten into Taiga's walk-in closet and was now wearing a brand-name overdress that probably cost one hundred thousand yen. Under that, of course, he had messily layered on a ton of fluffy lace underskirts that cost several tens of thousands of more yen.

What a huge idiot...

At the very moment everyone thought that, a small shadow flew through the air like a flying squirrel. That shadow quickly pulled the clothes off the idiot and slapped his cheeks.

"Ah! Ah!"

Then, as a finishing touch, the shadow hit him so hard with the corner of the computer that his head might have caved in.

"Everyone! We have to burn all these clothes to a crisp! They're biohazards!"

"Hey, hey, hey!" said Ryuuji. "That's a waste—*mottainai!* What do you think you're saying? Haruta just wore them for a second! Actually, more importantly, you idiot! Computers aren't blunt weapons! Are you sure you didn't break it?!"

"Calm down, it's the type of computer where you can drop it from two meters and it'll be fine."

"Taka-chan...were...weren't you supposed to be worrying about me?" Tears came spewing from Haruta's eyes.

The members of the group addressed Haruta in gentle voices:

"You're the one who was wrong."

"You reap what you sow."

"I'd rather you stay unconscious."

Holding the printer, Minori inferred what happened to Haruta and offered him a silent prayer.

"Now, Haruta's quieted down, so let's start making the school trip guidebook! All together now! Bow!"

When it came to taking charge, Kitamura had no competition. They all bowed and clapped.

"It needs to be on B5-sized paper and six pages long, not including the cover sheet. Four pages need to be research done prior to the trip...and that's the part we're going to work on now. I drew from other guidebooks by researching the history of the land. For the rest of the book, we can write our own impressions. Apparently, we're going to put them all together for the whole school's class yearbook, and then we're giving copies to the parents. I was thinking we could at least use it as a reference, so I borrowed last year's book."

"Nothing less expected from the master! Good job! If we just copy this, we probably wouldn't even get caught, right?"

"Huh? Noto, of course we couldn't do that. What's the use of copying the history of Okinawa? Are you like actually a super big idiot?" Maya was cold to Noto.

They opened the booklet and peeked into it.

"Ahhh..." Their listless voices rang out at practically the same time.

The third years' memories of Okinawa were just too dazzling for them. The research pages were nothing, but the impressions pages were so blinding it made their eyes squint. The skies and seas were so blue they didn't seem real, and the beach was a glittering pure white. They had gone the year before in the middle of winter in January as well, but everyone was wearing merry Uminchu calligraphy T-shirts, baseball caps, and had towels around their necks under the brilliant, glittering sun, with faces that said "It's hot!" "It's too bright!" They were slurping up Okinawa soba and nibbling on sata andagi doughnuts. There was even a picture of them on an isolated island like they had seen on TV, being pulled by buffalo.

"Ngh?!" Noto's voice suddenly went shrill. He slammed the book closed. They raised their faces in surprise to look at Noto. "N-nothing..."

He was being very suspicious.

"No, this isn't suspicious! But, we can't reference this anyway, so let's stop looking at it! Let's think about what we're actually going to do! Anyway, let's ask Google-sensei about something! Uhh, where's the computer's AC adapter..."

"Whaaat's going on, Noto-kun? What did you see just now? That was suuuper suspicious... It was right around this page, wasn't it?"

"Ah, wait a sec, Ami-chan!"

Ami stole the booklet from Noto where he sat across from her, with the low table between them. She grinned as she turned back to the earlier page. As long as it wasn't making the boring lame guidebook, anything probably would have been amusing to her.

"Oh! Oh my my my my! Oh my...so it's this."

"What is it?" said Kitamura. "Does it have anything to do with me?"

"Hey wait, just stop it," Noto whispered to Ami.

But Ami wasn't listening. She pouted happily and looked steadily at her childhood friend as she said in a low voice, almost as though speaking to herself, "Yuusaku's the only one I can't show this to."

"What... But actually, what is it? This is going to bother me. Let me see."

"Well, if you say so, Yuusaku, then I guess I've got to show you. I wonder what you'll think... Don't blame me if you end up crying..."

"Seems like you want me to... What's wrong with that picture of the buffalo—whoa!"

As soon as he looked at it, Kitamura froze. Everyone, wondering what it could possibly be, looked at it. Then they understood.

It was a picture of a certain group on a tour, being pulled by the buffalo as they crossed the remote island. Under the dazzling blue sky on the beach, a long-haired girl was left by herself on the luggage rack while everyone else walked happily into the shallows with the buffalo.

The girl left behind on the luggage rack had her hand on her hip and was laughing out loud. She seemed to arrogantly look on at the progress of things. It felt like they might hear her voice even now. *Daah ha ha ha ha ha haaa!* It was an incredibly manly voice and a hearty laugh.

In other words, the king on the luggage rack was everyone's former beloved patriarch, Kano Sumire.

"Whoa, that must be a shock. It must be, right? The person who so grandly rejected you in the end is suddenly right here in this picture. Poor Yuusaku, you okay?"

"Wh-why wouldn't I be?"

"So you're okay, that's good! Come to think of it, have you gotten any response from Kano-senpai? Maybe she's got a boyfriend in America right around now?"

"The president got to school...to MIT and was admitted... That's what I heard from her younger sister..."

"Huuh. So she's a university girl who skipped a grade! Aha! That's so cool! But what's Ehm Ah-ee Tee? Is it about as elite as Tokyo University in Japan? Is it like Ivy League? Yuusaku, why don't you just take the college entrance exams there, too? I've got no idea how American schools work!"

"...I wonder where the AC adapter is..."

Kitamura had been defeated by his childhood friend's merciless and completely obvious sadistic attack. He turned his back to everyone and started fiddling around with the computer cables that Taiga had brought in.

"I-Is this the AC adapter? I'm sure it must be this! And the socket, the socket... Where do you have a socket..." Noto, who started the whole mess, awkwardly stood up and began wandering around the condo.

"..."

Maya and Nanako were looking at each other with delicate expressions. For reasons no other person could fathom, Minori was sticking out her front teeth and looking at Kitamura from the corner of her eye. As for Taiga...

"Idiot! Idiot! Idiot! Idiot! You! Huge! Idiot!" she said in a low voice. She was hitting Ami with both her arms.

"What? I think it's his fault for being so depressed just because of that little thing. I was just making him stronger. Look, it's like Kaatsu training."

It seemed that Ami didn't care one bit that her childhood friend was feeling down. "Kaatsu!" she said as she gripped her hand into a fist.

Haruta finally came back to consciousness. "Where am I? Is this my room?"

He was the same as usual, no changes whatsoever.

As for Ryuuji, he passionately whispered to his friend in his mind, *I really understand how you feel.* Though Kitamura didn't know, they had both had their hearts broken. Little things could make their wounds reopen and sting. Ryuuji wasn't unfamiliar with that feeling.

"I'm going to put on the tea! Let's eat something and keep going! We can just relax and get things done! Okay!" he said with a loud cry and got up.

"I'm going to share these with everyone. They're madeleines from home. Actually, that seems like a lot for one person to handle? I, the wandering waitress Kushieda, shall help with something."

"Right, that'll be great. Could you look for cups for the tea? We need three more."

At the luxurious kitchen island that was installed at the back of the living room, Ryuuji's heart beat a little faster at the reinforcements that had arrived. He somehow calmed the beating in his chest.

Minori put the box of madeleines, which seemed to have been a gift, down in the kitchen. "Okay, okay," she answered and opened the cupboard to start rummaging through it.

"Hmmm, looks like there aren't any teacups. Would mugs work?"

"That'd be fine."

"Here ya go. Oh, this one's cute. It could hold a lot of tea. I'm going to call dibs on this one."

With expected skill, she grabbed three mugs in one hand and lined them up in front of Ryuuji. She poked at one with her fingertip. The large orange mug with a whale drawn on it was one which he was sure Taiga had gotten by collecting and trading in stickers from convenience store breads. Minori looked up at Ryuuji's face and grinned.

"What should we do with the madeleines? It's kind of too much to go as far as to put them on a plate. How about we just leave 'em in the box and slap them on the table?"

"I...I guess that's fine."

"I know, right?!"

She didn't notice Ryuuji suddenly staggering right next to her. He stood there almost defenselessly as they nearly rubbed elbows. She opened the package and the box.

"M-m-m-m-mado-ma-ma-ma-madole-l-l-l-l-l-lein."

Minori shook her butt and started rapping. She grabbed the individually wrapped madeleines one after another and put more and more of them out in a row on the marble counter.

"Wait...you...weren't you going to just slap them down in the box?"

"Hm?! Ohhh, you're right!"

Was she just on autopilot? Ryuuji watched Minori panic and put the madeleines back in the box. He wanted to laugh.

Compared to him, trying to hide his trembling fingers while he dropped tea bags into the cups, Minori's autopilot might have been an attempt to act natural. She was in an unfussy outfit that consisted of a zip-up parka and jeans. "Oh no, I wasn't thinking," she muttered. Her lips were flushed like a soft, light peach. Her round forehead, her cheeks, and her chin were, too.

"Hey, Golgo…"

"My name isn't Golgo…"

"Then I'll be Golgo… Don't stand behind me…"

"I'm not…"

Everything about her was pretty as always, and she had stolen his eyes. Minori stared at him, so Ryuuji put up both his hands, embarrassed, and turned his eyes away.

"Then fine… Actually, I broke the box when I opened it. We really do need a tray, I just saw one in here."

Minori smiled a little as she finished joking around. She seemed to be talking to herself as she opened the cupboard along the wall and brought out the silver tray she was looking for. "Hm, this is pretty heavy. Is this like a really good one? Is it expensive? I wonder if it's okay to use. Hey, Taiga."

Taiga immediately turned around to face her. Her tartan checked dress fluttered as she made her way to the kitchen.

"What's wrong? You need me for something?"

"This silver tray, can we use it? I want to bring out the madeleines on it."

"What? Of course you can use that thing. I thought there was something wrong."

"Well, look, sometimes these things can be shockingly expensive. That's what I was thinking. Hey, hey, actually—"

Minori lined the madeleines up on the tray as she suddenly grinned and looked at Ryuuji's face and Taiga's in turn.

"The cupboard and tableware are looking super organized. Takasu's been organizing things, and he's been doing such a great job. It's been a while since I've been here, and I'm just so impressed."

"It's tidy because I asked the Merry Maids to clean..."

Is it really? It is really. With the island kitchen between them, Minori and Taiga were posed in the same way, like sisters, and smiled as they looked at each other. *They really do get along,* Ryuuji thought as he poured hot water from the boiling T-Fal kettle into the cups. Before he realized it, he was completely out of the loop.

"But I think it's a big deal how Takasu-kun was managing things around here. It's been over a year since the last time I came by to clean things, right? You don't have as many unnecessary things, and it's gotten easier to keep up. That's all I'm saying. You have to make sure you show your appreciation to Takasu-kun."

"He just did it because he likes to. Like to the point he'd rather thank *me*, right Ryuuji?"

Taiga glanced at him, and he noticed her look.

This is a dangerous direction we're moving in, Taiga seemed to want to say. The course of the conversation was definitely progressing in the direction of "Taiga definitely needs Takasu-kun or she just can't make it." *Please do something.* Taiga's gaze was nervous and perplexed, but, to be honest, Ryuuji didn't know what to do.

"Well, it's definitely thanks to Takasu-kun. I know it! That's because I'm God!"

The only thing he could do was pretend to focus on making the tea and smile painfully. Now that Minori had said, *Because I'm God!* there was no way he could argue back.

"Aisaka, could I have a moment? We can't get online anymore. The wireless LAN is acting weird."

"Oh, really? But it was connected just now."

Help had been sent from heaven. Though it wasn't that serious of an issue, Kitamura had called Taiga over. With an obviously relieved expression, Taiga left the kitchen with Kitamura, who was wearing Uniqlo from head to toe as he did most days.

Minori, however, kept up the conversation with Ryuuji.

"I really do think that. Last year this place was filled with garbage, and no matter how many times I cleaned it, it wouldn't last a week. It was such a terrible mess!"

She kept talking without missing a beat. Ryuuji suddenly had a sense of incongruity.

"You hadn't come by this place for over a year even though you're so close?"

Come to think of it, hasn't Minori said something about this before?

"Well, that's—look...about before, with Taiga's dad, with what happened, I got in a fight with Taiga. We at least made up, but for some reason or another, since then... I didn't want to step in too close and make another mistake, since I didn't know what would happen. That's what I was thinking."

"Right... I remember now."

Ryuuji listened to Minori's words and automatically thought of himself. *Stepping in too close.* Wasn't that exactly what he was doing? Taiga was in the process of challenging herself to make it on her own, and she'd stopped coming over to his house or asking him to do chores for her.

"In other words, you did a good job...is what I want to say, Takasu-kun."

Minori hit him in the arm, like a guy would do to another guy. Normally, he would be happy at that touch, but right now, more importantly, how had he done a good job? He tried to ask her, but Minori was already starting to prepare the milk and sugar with her usual adeptness. As though trying to resolutely say, *Our conversation is over!* she turned her back to him.

Ryuuji closed his mouth. He wiped away the moisture in the kitchen with a dry towel. Everyone in the living room had abandoned the computer that wouldn't connect and started to chitchat. Kitamura and Taiga were the only ones attempting to turn the router set next to the wall on and off. They were seated on the carpet and working hard to somehow restart it.

Why you, Ryuuji suddenly thought. Just when had Taiga become able to sit that close to Kitamura? It was such a petty thought.

"Hey, Takasu-kun?"

"Don't stand behind me..."

"Don't steal my joke..."

Minori pushed her hair behind her ear and grinned. She was looking up at Ryuuji. He didn't know how long she had been watching him.

"So, um, about the school trip. I'm kind of looking forward to it... Actually, I'm really looking forward to it."

Hiding what was in his heart, Ryuuji scowled successfully. "Geh! Are you serious? We're just going skiing."

"I'm good at skiing. I'm like Shimizu Akira. And besides that, this is like the last of it. It's the last thing we're doing together as class 2-C. Ahh...this class was super fun, so I feel kind of lonely. Don't you feel like that, too?"

Checking how the tea was turning out, Minori half-closed her eyes and looked at the bottoms of the nine lined-up cups.

"I was thinking it'd be nice if everyone could always stay like this."

Always? Everyone? Like this? In other words—he grasped onto something but then got distracted.

From a ways away, Kitamura and Taiga's whispered conversation came to his ears by chance.

Really?

Yeah. So, I'd rather...

...then I'll...

Huh? Then...but why? Did something actually happen?

He didn't know what they were talking about, but it didn't seem like it was about the internet. Kitamura looked hurt. Taiga didn't falter or seem flustered as she looked into Kitamura's face.

She was smiling at him naturally in concern. She was peering into his eyes in worry.

The two of them looked natural as they drew near each other. They looked close—almost as though they had been close friends for years. *But really, at what point did she—*

"Right. Of course."

The part of the conversation he had caught disappeared as though it had been an unraveled knot.

"It'd be nice if it just stayed like this forever," Ryuuji answered, mostly unconsciously, and started to line up the saucers for the tea on the tray. He absorbed himself in the work.

Maybe the knot really had unraveled and disappeared, or tightened and tightened until it became so small it was invisible. No one knew which it was.

They collected information about the ski resort they were visiting and researched about the weather and the specialty products the region was known for. In the end, the nine of them didn't finish the pre-investigation on that Sunday but kept going until the next weekend. The honors student Kitamura had just been too full of vigor in the end.

Then, the days passed.

4

H E WOULD FIND OUT Minori's true feelings. Did Kushieda Minori really not want to date Takasu Ryuuji? Would her thoughts change if he stopped living with Aisaka Taiga?

He would ask her that and get an answer. If he could, he would also try once again to tell her about his feelings, like he had tried to before being interrupted on that Christmas Eve night. He could renew the relationship that had taken on such a delicate feeling.

For Ryuuji, that itself was the goal of this school trip.

"Takasu, you've got 'C,' okay? 'C.'"

"Confidence!"

"What was that?"

"We said we're only doing things that are bitter."

Booed at by all his classmates on the bus, Ryuuji cleared his throat in a fluster. "Uhhh, ah, 'cancer!' I think it'd taste bitter!

Okay, here, 'R!'" He gave the mic over to Taiga, sitting across the aisle from him.

"'R?!' ...Ramen...no, uhhh R...rhubarb! That's bitter, right?! Here, Minorin, you get 'B.'"

That was a nice answer. Taiga's "rhubarb" earned her applause.

It was the first day of the school trip.

Riding on six separate buses, the second years were heading to their final destination: the ski resort. However, the highway's incredibly boring scenery made people start to get carsick, so they had pulled out a mic in order to try doing karaoke, just to discover the machine only had ballads. In a fit of desperation, all of class 2-C started playing a game of limited *shiritori* to amuse themselves. They each went around saying a word that started with the last letter of the previous word that was said.

It really wasn't that great, and they could hardly say everyone was in a great mood, but it was leagues better than just watching the seemingly endless gray walls and gray roads.

"'B'...something that starts with 'B' and is bitter..."

Receiving the mic, Minori sat at her window seat with her knees drawn up. Wrinkles appeared on her forehead, and she groaned. Incidentally, the one who lost would have to sing their best karaoke ballad by themselves.

"Isn't Kushieda about to run out of time?"

"Okay, let's start the countdown! Ten! Nine! Eight! Seven! Six! Five! Four! Three! Two! One..."

As students started to clap their hands to the numbers, Minori suddenly took in a breath and went cross-eyed.

"BAAAAAAAAAAAAAAAAAAAAAAAM!" she yelled, veins throbbing on her forehead. The mic made a sound that was even past a screech, and it echoed unnecessarily in the bus.

"My ears!"

"Shuddup!"

"You think you're Moguro?!"

The students were in agony. Without minding them, Minori took the mic in her right hand as her left trembled.

"Right then, I felt a shock hit me like a wall of pressure, and for some reason, I have no idea why, but my eyes opened wide and I couldn't say anything. But why? But why was *it* here?"

She was channeling who knows what. Her voice was like the footsteps of a goblin scrambling past you in a corridor, and she breathed heavily into the mic as she blurted out words.

"Why...is...it...here? But didn't I just throw it away? I even offered a memorial service at the temple. I even put my hands together and begged for forgiveness. But then why is that doll back in my room? I would never bring that thing back, but there it is, right before my eyes! I put my hands together in spite of myself and started to pray, 'Please don't come back anymore. You don't belong here. You don't need to protect me anymore.' When I did that, the doll's empty eye sockets were too terrifying for me to look at, and in that moment, I felt like it was definitely looking back at me. I was in a panic. Stop. Please stop. Please, please. Stop

stop stop stop stop stop stop stop! Don't look at me! No no no no no no no no NO NO NO NO NO NO NO NO NO NO NO NO NO NO NO NO! DON'T LOOOOOOOK!"

When she shook the seat in front of her as part of her passionate performance, the girl sitting there started to scream. Next to her, Taiga's eyes were full of tears. Even Ryuuji gulped, scooting away with his hand on his mouth like a little grandmother. He was speechless. *Sure, I wanted to ask you what your true feelings were, but no one asked you—*

"'*YOU* ARE THE ONE WHO DOES NOT BELONG!'"
"AHHHHHHH!" "NOOOOOOOOOOOO!"
—for a friggin' ghost story.

In the pandemonium and agonized screams that ensued, Ryuuji squeezed his eyes tight. Taiga let out a little "Eek..." and covered her ears.

"Your story isn't scary! *You're* just scary with your voice and how you act!" Kitamura declared. Ryuuji was on the same page as he looked at Minori. However, she didn't seem to have a single regret as she stuck out her tongue and grinned in satisfaction.

"So, your letter is 'G.' Here, Ahmin."

"How was that bitter?!"

"That was a bittersweet, true story about my doll."

She stood on her knees in her seat and handed off the mic to Ami, directly behind her. It probably wasn't because of the story, but Ami was currently in a bad mood. She roughly brushed up her long hair as she took the mic. Her lips twisted spitefully.

Ami had actually tried to skip the school trip, but when she told the bachelorette (age 30) that she would be taking an absence for work, she was apparently breezily rejected because, "You're a student, so your school trips are top priority!" Because she had already used work as an excuse, she didn't have any other way of ditching and had to come in the end.

"'G,' huh?! How about 'Guess what my mood is right now'! Here, Maya! You've got 'W'!"

Good letter! Nice answer! You're always the best, Ami-chan! There was applause, but something as little as that couldn't fix Ami-chan-sama's mood. Still looking sour, she stuck her face into the curtain that hung on the window and sulked.

"What?! 'W'...wooly mammoth boiled in absinthe."

"Kihara...what do you mean, 'What?!' Your thing is weirder!"

"Maybe that warrants a countdown?!"

Maya wailed, "You mean you're okay with Kushieda's ghost story and Ami-chan's mood, but my wooly mammoth doesn't count?!" However, there was no fair judge around for her. No one, not even Ryuuji, wanted to give the mic back to Minori, and they were all privately in agreement that that no one wanted to provoke Ami when she was overflowing with irritation, plus...

"I wanna hear your solo, Maya-sama! Heh heh heh!"

A lot of guys nodded at Haruta's words, which he practically sang as he crinkled his nose.

"What?! That's not even funny! Besides, people probably did boil mammoths in absinthe! They probably did?!"

The bus went into a tunnel. *Nuh-uh!* Ryuuji tried to retort at Maya's nonsense, but his ears popped, and he scowled.

The tunnel was short. They immediately caught sight of a point of light ahead that grew as they approached it.

"What?!" The first person to exclaim was Maya, who still had the mic.

Ryuuji saw white as the strong rays of light showered him. He tried checking to see what it could have been but had to swallow his breath at how blinding it was.

"No way! It's snow! Snow! Look, snow! Why are we playing this game?! This is amazing!"

At Maya's loud screams, even Ami opened her eyes wide and jumped up. Ryuuji and the others stood up from their seats, and with one look at the scene beyond the window, began exclaiming like children, "Whoa, cool!"

So far, they had seen grayish-black snow built up under the dirty guardrails, but this wasn't anything like that. Ryuuji and Kitamura were cheek to cheek and pressed up against the window. They were exclaiming like girls.

"Cool, cool, cool! What's that glittering there?! It's sunny out, so it can't be snowing—"

"Precisely! That *is* snow! Whoa! It's suddenly like *Snow Country!* Amazing!"

The scene beyond the windows was magnificent.

They bustled around, exclaiming at how amazing it was, and the ones with window seats opened their windows one after another.

The cold but refreshing air suddenly filled the bus, and they breathed it in. Their eyes glittered as though they were coming back to life.

Beyond the tunnel, everything everywhere was white, white, white. It glittered, like a world cast from silver. The light from the snow was dazzling, a scene outside of their normal lives.

"Whoa!" Taiga yelled. "This is the first time I've seen anything like this!"

She stuck her face out the window with Minori. *This is Taiga we're talking about,* Ryuuji thought. *She might just tumble right out.* But Minori had a firm hold of the back of Taiga's jacket. He saw that and felt relieved.

"It's soooooo pretty! Whoa, I feel so excited!"

"Isn't it kinda hot for being a snowy mountain?!"

"This is snow country! It really is!"

"Whoa! Those mountains over there are all white! Cool!"

"Ahhhhhhhh! Gotta get a picture! Let's take one together!"

The mountain range that the boisterous class's bus was heading towards was white and glittered divinely. It looked gallant with its crown of snow. The remarkably tall summit, piercing the heavens, was bathed in golden sunlight.

What? It's better than I thought! This is completely fine! It's super great! The hearts of everyone in 2-C had become one.

Without hesitation, the bachelorette (age 30) sitting in the very front turned around in excitement and pointed at the peak as she proclaimed, "Now everyone, are you finally excited now?! We're heading to that mountain! Ready?!"

YAHOOOOOOOOOOOOOOOOOOOOOOOOOOOOOO!

Their voices and hearts were one. They cheered and applauded as the bus driver mumbled incoherently, "We're not going to *that* mountain..."

"This is so unfair... How do you look so good in that?"

"You think I look good? Me? Well, I guess I'm the type of person who just looks good in anything that looks like a tracksuit."

At the gathering area, Kitamura was checking out his own rental gear as Noto looked at him with obvious jealousy. Rather than normal purple or any sensible color, the shade of his ridiculous top and bottom was something that one could really only describe as "flamboyant purple." On the chest of his top and the hem of his pants, there were lines in lightning designs that really couldn't be called gold so much as "flamboyant yellow." That was the kind of snow gear he had on. On top of that, the material seemed satin-like... Well, because it *was* satin.

As if that wasn't bad enough, all of them even had competition bib numbers on their chests. Were they white, you ask? Ridiculous. They were turquoise, naturally. It seemed that turquoise was the color of class 2-C. The other classes that gloomily passed by them were dealing with their own ordeals and had numbers that were in green, maroon, and crimson.

How does he look like that even in ski gear like this? Ryuuji thought. Kitamura, who stood in his rented boots on top of the packed down snow path, looked pretty slick. It might have been because of his physique or because of the PE blood that raced through him, but he made the uniform look as though it could actually have belonged to a real competitive ski team. It was scarily believable. If anything, Ryuuji and Noto were in agreement—Kitamura was unfair.

The moment they arrived at the hotel, they were each given one of those cruel outfits and put in rooms that were divided by gender. (Those rooms were also beyond description, though to put it simply, they were Japanese-style rooms that would make Minori drool.) They got changed and were made to gather as a class at the entrance to the ski slopes, which was near the entrance of the hotel.

"Takasu, you kind of look ridiculous..."

"Don't say it. I know."

At Noto's look, which was apologetic, Ryuuji bit his lip. If he smiled, he was a devil. If he cried, he was a demon. If he opened his mouth, he was a wanted criminal. There was no way gear in these insane colors would ever work with the face he had. It was like he was a doll with an interchangeable head. The closest anyone could get to describing it was "like a Thai drag queen hitman whose makeup has completely come off by the end of a battle."

Incidentally, Noto looked like a worn-out ventriloquist's doll used to explain traffic safety.

"Hah! I've figured out why Kitamura looks so good in it! It's the knit cap and the goggles he's got around his neck! Noto, Taka-chan, we've got to copy him!"

Haruta, who had started a meaningless tirade of serious non-sense, looked like a fashionable boy who had accidentally been sent to juvie. It was pretty tragic. But somehow, just as the idiot had said, when they all put on the hats they had brought with them and put their goggles around their necks...

"..."

"..."

"..."

Each member of the trio frowned at how the others looked. Something was wrong. There was something so evidentially different between them and the girls' favorite, Maruo-kun, but hurting each other wouldn't help anyone.

It was fine. Even if they looked lame or scary, it wasn't as though they were trying to pass themselves off as cool in the first place. Ryuuji turned away and took in a deep breath of the chilly mountain air. The air was fresh, as expected. The cold and clear chill felt good in his lungs, and he felt like the carsickness that had faintly followed him cleared up, like taking a Quickle Wiper to the floor.

There was a pile of snow about as tall as a person by the wall that held the entrance to the slopes. The other guys in the class were making a big deal out of trying to eat it, and he saw skiers who seemed to be locals unable to stop themselves from laughing, "That stuff's as dirty as the rest of it."

They were embarrassing even though they were high school students—though if no one were looking, Ryuuji would have tried eating the snow, too.

Actually, there wasn't any point in pretending this wasn't the first time Ryuuji had gone skiing. Of course, he hadn't seen such huge masses of snow before, either. He hadn't known that snow could be so blinding.

The scene, without complaints, was grand. He swore on the mama's boy star that he wouldn't forget to take a picture later to show Yasuko.

Around that time, the girls also started wandering in, and Ryuuji and the rest of the boys forgot what they looked like as they pointed and laughed.

"Bwah!"

"Ha ha ha, what're you wearing?!"

"This is the worst..."

"Bwah ha!"

Taiga appeared in front of Ryuuji's eyes with her long hair in braids. She looked angry enough she could die, and Ryuuji finally let out a laugh.

It was mind-numbingly pink...no, it was hot pink! Plus emerald green that made one want to just pinch their eyes shut... no, it was EM-ER-ALD! GREEN! As though trying to elicit the feeling of speed, each of the girls' uniforms had a curved line that went from left shoulder to right foot. Of course, the material was kind of satiny... Well, it was actually just satin. On top of that, all of class 2-C had their turquoise numbers.

The boys' uniforms were something, but this was just a debacle. It was a modern jumpsuit design, and the waistline, well, was an abomination. On top of that, Taiga's already petite frame meant that she was practically swimming in her gear, and she was about seventeen times larger than normal. If a strong enough wind came by, she'd probably float right up into the mountains like Mary Poppins. That would be an unexpectedly mournful way to part.

The year's school trip gear was in such bad taste that the gods of the distant mountain ranges might be pointing and laughing at them.

"Hee hee hee hee! That's so...hee hee hee!"

"What're you laughing about?! This isn't a laughing matter!"

Taiga was already on the verge of hysterics. She stamped her feet.

"How do they expect us to snow ski on the ski snowpes—the ski swopes—the ski soaps—how do they expect us to go out on the snow hills while retaining our dignity in this?! Is this going to be preserved in a group picture?! If I'm involved in a crime in the future, is this insane outfit going to be televised all over the country and published in newspapers and magazines and conserved for eternity?! Urgh! Just putting it into words is terrifying! Ahhh!"

"Don't commit that crime, then..."

"Victims end up in the news, too! If the world suddenly sees me like this...huh?! What are *you* wearing?! You're...bwah ha!"

Taiga looked at Ryuuji and burst out laughing as she collapsed. *Laugh all you want*—Ryuuji was serene. Taiga looked just as ridiculous, and so her laughter didn't hurt him. Plus, the air was nice. The scenery was amazing.

The blue sky didn't have a single cloud.

The slope started where the entrance to the stops was, and they could see a large lodge halfway down. It was connected to a slow-moving lift, and the descending skiers and boarders left beautifully meandering lines behind them in the white snow.

The slopes, which were mostly deserted, glittered brightly.

"Hey, you guys! Don't underestimate the mountain! And don't be charmed by a mountain boy! Whoa?!" Minori, who followed after Taiga, was speechless at the boys' attire. "Whoa! The boys are in colors that make my eyes bleed, too...ahhh!"

Ryuuji, and everyone else, were rendered speechless as Minori slipped and fell right over. She hadn't even fallen because the packed snow had turned to ice and gone slippery.

"Ouch! Hey! Who was eating the banana?!"

At her feet...or rather, at her butt, was a banana peel.

"Minorin, are you okay?! Can you stand?! Are you hurt?!"

Then Taiga tried to lend her a hand, and it probably wasn't just Ryuuji who was waiting for the next thing to happen.

"Oh no, Minorin's butt is broken...ahh!"

"Ahhhh..."

Trying to get up at the same time as Minori, Taiga, who was basically guaranteed to do something klutzy, slipped. They tumbled magnificently to their butts at the same time and began to slide right down the icy slope while screaming at the top of their lungs.

"Wait! Wait! Wait! No way! Get away, get away, get away!"

"No, stop! That's dangerous!"

Taiga and Minori careened into the trio of beautiful girls who had been standing ahead of them, sending them flying into a soft snowdrift, and then came to a halt.

"T-Tiger and Kushieda! What do you think you're doing?!"

"Ugh! This is embarrassing and cold..."

"S-s-s-s-sorry Maya-sama and Nanako-sama! Please, take my hand! I'm so sorry, Ahmin! Are you okay?"

Minori bent down to lend a hand to the three. Maya and Nanako, covered with snow, hoisted themselves up.

"Ahmin? Hey, what's wrong?"

There was one girl who did not get up.

Face smushed directly into the snow and her butt sticking straight up, Ami didn't so much as twitch.

"Dammit, she's dead, Jim," Taiga muttered, and Haruta beside her shrieked, "PEEE-KYAAA!" He wasn't letting a lightning bolt loose. It seemed he just thought it was funny.

"Oh no. Ami might not be able to stand because she's lost the will to live!" Maya said as she stared at Ami's butt. Nanako also nodded.

"It's 'cause the clothes are so lame. We even had to carry her here."

That's idiotic... Ryuuji thought to himself.

Ami's childhood friend, Kitamura, stepped in. "Okay! Having her in this position is kind of risky, so no one else get involved!"

He firmly grasped Ami's on-all-fours form and yelled, *Upsy daisy!* Then he hoisted her buried body out of the snow. He even batted off the snow stuck to her head.

"Ami! Keep it together! Are you okay?!"

"Where am I...? What happened...? Am I dying...?"

Dressed in the terrible uniform, Ami looked lifeless. Neither her goody-two-shoes mask nor her true dark underside were showing. Her eyes were empty, and her mouth was half-open.

"Oh! She really has lost her will to live, poor thing..."

"Anyone have a marker? If we draw a Chanel mark on her clothes, Dimhuahua will come back to life." Taiga's eyes were serious as she searched for a bold-tip marker.

"Okay! We've got everyone here! Please get right into your groups and form a line! Bwah ha!"

All of their eyes suddenly turned in one direction. Before them was the bachelorette (age 30), also known as Koigakubo Yuri. She was the only one in her own clothing, in fashionable snowboarding gear—and on top of that, it was white! Shameless! She was desperately keeping her gaze on the ground.

"Everyone...you've got some amazing gear on...I couldn't have imagined this..."

The students stared back at her, lined up in their intense purple and hot pink with turquoise on the side, and Koigakubo Yuri couldn't keep her laughter to herself. The giggles she couldn't stifle began to spill from behind the attendance sheet she hid behind.

Correctly intuiting the class's will, Kitamura became the champion of a revolution. Ami stood up with a dark grudge in her eyes. *Aim for the skies, down with the castle.* Kitamura raised his right arm.

"Ready your aim!"

All of 2-C took snow from their feet. They packed it together in their hands.

"Huh? What? No! What are you doing? Huh?"

"Fire!"

At Kitamura's command, they all released their snowballs and hit the bachelorette (age 30) without mercy. The other classes and general skiers pointed and laughed.

After they had all finished their greetings and warm-ups, the second-year students scattered in groups, creating pink and purple dots on the gentle snow slopes. In preparation for taking on the full-scale practice courses after lunch, they were spending an hour beforehand getting used to the snow and figuring out what their individual levels were.

The nine-person group that Kitamura led was on the vast, expansive slopes on the gentle foot of the mountain as they put on their ski gear.

"Oh! I-I'm starting to move! What am I supposed to do?!"

It was the first time Ryuuji had put on skis, and though he had just barely prepared himself, he started to slip down the slope while still half-bent over.

"You need to be perpendicular to the slope!" Kitamura quickly advised him.

"Huh?! Perpendicular?! But how…ahhh?!"

"Use your poles! If that doesn't work, you can sit down! Just keep calm and don't hurt your knees! Put your weight in front of you!"

"Huuuh…whoa?!"

He couldn't use the two poles, which just flailed in the air. The more his skis slid, the further his legs separated, until he was doing the splits. Ryuuji started to panic that he'd hurt himself, lost his balance, and flipped over magnificently.

"This isn't fun!"

He looked at his two skis, which were reaching up to the blue skies, and groaned.

"It's been too long! This snow's pretty nice! Oh, oh. There, there. Oh, oh, oh, oh."

Perched on a section of hard snow that had been packed into a mound, Minori was shuffling her weight forward and back as though testing the snow. Then she lined up her skis perfectly and thrust, twisting her hips above the mound, and jumped several times to the left and right.

Ryuuji had no idea what she was trying to do, but eventually, Minori yielded to the mound and fwooshed forward a short distance. She sent snow flying as she stopped herself. She had perfectly controlled her skis by only shifting her weight.

She looked unusually cool when she did that. Ryuuji forgot that he was still sitting down, unintentionally captivated at how confident Minori was with her skis. Her beanie rested lightly on her head, and her short hair was forced into a ponytail so it poked out at the bottom. That was also so unusually cute that Ryuuji already couldn't take his eyes off her.

From a short distance away, as though acting as a spokesperson for Ryuuji's feelings, Ami patted her gloved hands together in applause.

"Minori-chan, you've got that handled! You're great at skiing! Wouldn't expect less from our all-around athlete!"

"Heh heh, you think so? Actually, aren't you pretty good, too?"

"What, me? No way! I'm just average!"

I'm average! Ami kept saying as she smoothly pushed herself forward on a mostly flat area of snow as though she were skating. She hummed as she leaned her weight on one leg and curved around, almost like she was doing an elegant dance, to return to them. If that really was just "average," then what did that make him when he couldn't even stand up? Was he just an abnormality? A fluke?

Ryuuji was trying to get up, but when he moved his feet, his skis knocked together, and the curves at the tips tangled in each other so he got locked into place. To top it off, the backs of his skis were stuck in the snow, and he couldn't move no matter what he did. He got tired and tried to turn over on the snow. His lameness was probably on another level.

As he breathed and lifted his face awkwardly, he saw Maya and Nanako happily laughing.

"Like a V...like a V...oh, I'm doing it! Aren't I pretty good?!"

"I wonder if I can do it if it's just a bend. I haven't been skiing since I was a first-year in junior high, but it's like riding a bike."

Even they were sliding around like they knew what they were doing. Like Minori, Kitamura, and Ami, it seemed Maya and Nanako also had experience with skiing.

Maybe he was the only one in the group who didn't know how? If that were the case, he felt pretty left out. He wanted there to be another beginner like him. The moment he thought that...

"Huh? What are you sitting around for, Takasu? Let's go ski!" Though he was a little unsteady, Noto also slipped by ahead of him. The light from the snow reflected off his glasses. Then, after him...

"I'm really a lot better at snowboarding."

His long hair fluttering audaciously, even Haruta looked cool as he slid by. He seemed to be having fun. Ryuuji was using all his willpower to keep the evil eye in his forehead from opening when he remembered—now that he thought of it, hadn't Haruta said his grandfather lived right next to a ski resort?

He felt incredibly left behind. *Traitors*, he muttered as he stared at his friends. He accidentally lost hold of one of his poles and quickly tried to grab on to its strap, but it slid down the gentle slope much faster than expected. He couldn't even stand, much less go after it. He quickly followed the direction it headed with his eyes.

"Oh, lost object spotted!"

The snow scattered as someone made a tight and elegant turn.

Minori grabbed the sliding pole and lifted her goggles up. She was always this enthusiastic whenever it came to sports.

"Is this yours, Takasu-kun? You've got to put this strap around your wrist!"

She sounded a bit condescending as she lectured him. Her face seemed too vivid, and he felt like he might be blinded. Coupled with the blazingly bright slopes, Minori really seemed to sparkle and glitter while standing in the middle of the snow.

"Hey there! You listening?! Look, hold your pole properly now!"

"Uhhh... Sorry!"

As though he were being drawn into her smile, Ryuuji unconsciously stood himself up on the slope using only his remaining pole. *Huh, I can stand. Maybe I'll be able to just start skiing like this right away?* But the moment he thought that...

"Whoa?!"

Schloop! His skis started sliding down the slope toward Minori. He waved his one hand and pole around as he tried to regain his balance. His legs were incredibly jerky, and his skis were going in completely different directions as he went forward.

"Ahh!"

"Okay! Just jump into my open arms!" Minori boldly stretched her arms out in front of him.

"Ahhhh! S-sorry! I'm ashamed of myself!"

"Oof! It's okay... Don't worry about it!"

Nothing could have been more awkward.

He had pretty much run straight into Minori, which stopped him firmly in his tracks. They lay down on the hard snow together for a while.

"I'm really sorry..."

"Uh! Really, don't worry about it!"

"Sorry, I'm sorry, I'm so sorry, ahh...I'm really so sorry..."

The more he apologized, the more awkward it became. Minori was still on the ground, and his demonic face was pressed a little too close to her chest, and Ryuuji couldn't stand up. The more he panicked, the more their skis clunked into each other. At least it was lucky for him that neither of them could feel anything beyond their gear (like really, really lucky!).

"Takasu-kun, you really don't need to worry about it, but you also really don't need to panic either."

"No no no, s-s-s-sorry! I'll get up right now! Just wait a second!"

"Actually...whenever you move your skis, you're really giving my butt a wedgie..."

"Ahhhhh! Noooooo!"

He couldn't fathom where the brute strength came from, but Ryuuji pulled himself away immediately. He jumped back from Minori, his face as red as a devil's as he hid his burning cheeks with his gloves. He sat with his legs folded to the side on the slopes and wriggled in embarrassment.

"H-how could I have... This is too embarrassing... I'm done for! I can't live anymore! You can leave me behind here! Please!"

"I'm the one who's more embarrassed! Anyway, it doesn't matter, so just stand up! Okay?!"

"Huh?!"

Lightly skating, Minori came around to Ryuuji's back and stuck her hands under his arms. *Up you go!* The moment she pulled him up, she balanced Ryuuji so he was upright.

"Wh-whoa, wait... I'm moving! I'm moving!"

"Oh, that was close... Oh, but see, you can slide! Keep it going!"

"No! I'm not skiing, I just can't stop!"

With Minori supporting him from the back, they slid down the slopes while lined up with each other.

"Now you've got to get used to balancing like this! We're going to keep going like this for a while!"

"You serious?!"

Still holding on to Ryuuji under his armpits, Minori skillfully threw her poles onto the ground one at a time. She straddled Ryuuji's skis with her own, keeping her balance firm. Ryuuji's knees naturally relaxed and bent forward.

"Whoa...oh oh ohhh..."

For the first time in his life, he cut through the wind on skis. Surprisingly easily, the four skis seemed to dance as they went down the rough slopes. *I see—because my ankles are supported by the boots, I need to use my knees to ski smoothly.* His body understood the logic behind it, but not the rest of him.

"Oh oh ahhhh! I-I'm definitely scared!"

"It'll be fine. You can't go fast on slopes like these! Careful not to get tangled up with me!"

"Ahhhhhh! Whoa!"

"Actually, you're really good! When I started skiing as a third grader, my dad taught me like this, too!"

"B-but...it's sort of embarrassing for me!"

"Why would it be?!"

"Because I'm not a third-grade girl, and you're not my dad!"

"Ha ha ha! Good one! Another!"

Another what?! Ryuuji's reply was blown away in the wind. They really were going pretty slow as they kept their skis in a V shape together while sliding down the slope. Little by little, he did feel like he was getting used to balancing.

At the same time, though, rather than nerves or invigoration, a lot of other, much more turbulent things started swirling in his mind.

For example, the feeling of the hands under his arms. And the breath he could feel immediately behind him.

"..."

He started wondering why she had only been willing to grab the edge of his sleeve earlier, when she was so willing to accompany him so closely today. He felt like no one would go to lengths like these if they hated the person they were with, and then he wondered what kind of look she had on her face in that moment.

"Hey! Don't you think you can ski by yourself soon?! Should I let go?! Are you okay?!"

Then he thought, maybe he really could expect a different answer from the one she had given on the night of Christmas Eve.

"K-Ku-shieda..."

I want to know what your true intentions are, what your real feelings—

"Ahhh, wait?! Don't turn around!"

"Whoa?!"

They lost their balance and veered. In that moment, their skis clattered and tangled together. Before they knew it, Minori was on her side and Ryuuji was on his butt as they tumbled down the slope.

Even though it was snow, they hit the ground pretty hard, and the breath was knocked out of them for a moment.

"Ouch...are you okay?!" Ryuuji panicked a bit as he looked for Minori.

"Oww...I'm okay! I'm okay! I'm completely fine!"

She patted the snow off her gear and got up right behind him. She put her beanie back on as she looked back at Ryuuji.

"If you come out to ski, you have to expect little bumps! This was easy! Look, now stand up on your own!"

Like a teacher, she suddenly pointed at him. She didn't even wait for Ryuuji to stand up as she turned to the skies and spread out her arms in a sweeping gesture. "Ahh!"

"Ah well! It was going great though! Actually, I seem to be missing my poles..."

She looked quizzically at her own empty hands. Ryuuji felt like he was going to fall over again.

"You're the one who threw your own poles down!"

"Oh, you're right! Oh no, when I grabbed yours, I left mine behind. Am I an idiot? I'm going to get them back!"

Minori started to skillfully go back up the gentle slope with her skis still on and without her poles, as though she were walking. She left a reverse V behind her in the snow as she went.

Left behind, Ryuuji simply watched her back. Incidentally, he still hadn't figured out how to stand up.

He did feel like he was doing good, though not in the way Minori had meant. He felt like things would turn out fine.

Then again, maybe expecting things to keep going well was foolish. He was just being audacious for a boy who'd been rejected. He looked around at his current situation, left behind, and decided to make sure he didn't anticipate too much. He would do his best to pretend he didn't notice the faint hope that came bubbling up inside him.

He breathed in and scowled. He took off the skis that were useless when he used them alone. However, his thoughts were already jittering, floating, and overeager in their turmoil. That was bad. He wouldn't be able to really listen to what Minori actually wanted if he was in such high hopes.

"Whoa?!"

Ryuuji was sent flying forward by a sudden impact. His face was thrust right into the snow, and he raised his head to figure out what was going on.

"Don't just stand there, you useless doll!"

He realized he had been run over.

There was Taiga—smugly straddling a sled. Taiga, who was apparently recklessly sledding down the slopes, glared at Ryuuji with her face contorted into a brutal expression. Still on the ground, he was unable to quickly come up with anything to say back at her.

"You...really...you're...actually...you've...seriously...you..."

"Huh? What're you saying? Ugh, bleh! You're in the way! I was going down so great, and now you've made me stop!"

Taiga sat back down on her red plastic sled, paddling forward with her rudely splayed legs. She got a little momentum and the sled started sliding down.

"Whoa..."

"Hmph!"

She ran over Ryuuji, who was in front of her, again.

"Seriously, what are you actually doing? Why're you under my sled?"

"You-you-you...why you!"

As he stood up, Ryuuji snapped.

"What's with *you*?! Why are you like that?! Why're you running me over?! Don't do that! I don't want to be run over!" he wailed as he approached Taiga.

"Ew...what're you yelling at me for? Did something bad happen to you? Okay, fine. I'll hear you out on what happened, just this once."

Taiga shrugged her shoulders, pretending to look wise.

"What happened?" She arrogantly thrust out her chin and even had a magnanimous smile playing across her face.

It was just the way she said that and the look on her face...

NGAAAAAAAH. Ryuuji squeezed out a scream of a kind that had never come from him before. If he were an American, he'd say "Goddamn!" If he were Chinese, "AIAHHHH!" In Ryuuji's case though, it was "NGAAAAAH." He held his head in his hands and then flung them up as he yelled as loud as he could.

"Something did happen! I got run over! Plus! You did it twice!"

"It wasn't like I said I wanted to ride a sled." Still perched right on the sled, Taiga put her chin in her hand and started to tell Ryuuji about something that had nothing to do with his anger. Ryuuji was about to tell her that her ears might as well belong in the trash if she wasn't actually going to listen.

"After I rented my skis, but before I got up here, I dropped them twice, and they hit the bachelorette (age 30) both times. So I went to grab the skis the second time, and when I turned around to follow everybody, I hit her with the skis again."

"Th...that's something..."

What she had to say actually seemed to be something worth listening to. He would never approach Taiga while she held anything long after this.

"So I was banned from having skis. They told me it was too dangerous and to use a sled instead. I was like, 'Is that something a teacher should be saying to her student?' Well, I can't ski anyway, and our gear looks like this, so I told her I didn't care anymore."

TORADORA!

"What?!" Ryuuji unintentionally yelled. He pointed at Taiga, and his eyes suddenly sparkled. "You can't ski!"

"Why are you so happy all of a sudden? Ew!"

The back of his head still hurt from being run over, but at least something had come of it. He had found someone else who couldn't ski. That was right—he had forgotten about the klutziest tiger in the whole world. Taiga.

"I thought I was the only one who couldn't ski in our group. You're part of the can't-ski team!"

"Huh?! No way! I thought Minorin and Kitamura would obviously be able to, but everyone else can, too?! Even that idiot?!"

"Take a look at that agile form."

Blergh! Taiga looked at Haruta, who was skiing lightly before her eyes, and wailed. She rubbed her eyes as though she were in a manga.

"The world is coming to an end...ahhh. Skiing is boring. Why would anyone wear those long things on purpose and try sliding around on the snow in the first place? It's not like we live in a place where it snows. I just don't get it."

"Same. Well...we can't keep complaining. How about you just ask Kitamura nicely to show you? He's a devil of a teacher, so he'll probably really beat it into you."

"How would he teach me anything about sledding?"

When she said it out loud, he had to agree. Taiga had a very strong air of persuasion as she sat enshrined on that bright red sled.

"How about you lead by example and go ask Minorin to teach you?"

"Unfortunately, she already did. And then when she left me, you chose that moment to bestow your presence upon me and ran me over. Now I've even lost the opportunity to go after her."

"What? Don't blame anyone else for your own mistakes, you mood killer." Taiga turned away and huffed out a white cloud. "Seriously... The way you're going, me trying to live on my own is going to amount to nothing."

Come to think of it... Ryuuji remembered something.

He felt like it had been a while since he and Taiga had talked alone together like this. Not so long ago, they had been like this every morning and every night. Just having a little argument like this made the abdominal muscles he normally didn't use feel tight and tired.

"Right... It's been a lot longer than I thought."

Ever since he was hospitalized—in other words, ever since Minori rejected him on that Christmas Eve, Taiga had cut off her contact with Ryuuji cold turkey. Of course, they saw each other at school, but they really hadn't been together face-to-face in a while.

"You're really getting into it, too."

At Ryuuji's words, Taiga puffed out her chest and arrogantly swept aside one of her braids.

"That's right! And I'm going to keep going like this for my whole life! So you should work harder in order to show your gratitude for how considerate I'm being! Well...it's not like I'm trying to live on my own for your sake. In the end, it's for myself."

It's practice for living by myself and becoming an adult.

She continued, "Okay, so anyway, get back! I'll run you over again if you don't!"

"So you were doing it on purpose?!"

"Well, it's just a figure of speech."

Taiga had a wicked little grin on her face as she began to paddle the sled with her legs. She then started to slide down the gentle sloping hills as she gained momentum.

"Whoa?!"

It might have been divine punishment. Before Ryuuji's eyes, her sled turned itself head over heels. The snow she had flung up scattered in intense contrast against the blue sky.

"How?!" Taiga yelled.

"You...fell over on your sled. Just how..."

"Ouch! Eek, that was a surprise! I just went too fast!"

He half dragged his heavy boots as he ran closer and righted the tipped sled. He also tried to help up Taiga, who was covered in snow.

"I don't need you!"

Her words were simple. Taiga hoisted herself up on her own and slapped off the snow on her gear. Then, she straddled the sled again.

"You know what...I think there's something super dangerous about you sledding on your own. Maybe you should give it a rest?" Ryuuji had automatically stepped on the back of the sled to stop it.

Taiga turned around and clicked her tongue. She contorted her face and glared at Ryuuji.

"Shut up! I said I'm fine! Let go! Get off!"

"No, but I can see it... I can see you sliding down the hill in the sled, not being able to stop, and then hitting the wall of the lodge and breaking a bone and crying... If that happened, that bone would hurt for the rest of your life when it's raining, cold, or hot... That'll definitely happen...and it'll be a pity."

"You..."

Taiga opened her eyes eerily wide at Ryuuji. She seemed a little taken aback. She scowled.

"You've got some nerve pretending to care about me while you're imagining something as ominous as that..."

"But it really could happen. Especially to a klutz like you."

"I said I'm fine! I don't need you taking care of me anymore! Just get your stinking foot out of the way already!" Taiga yelled as though she were about to snap and paddled as hard as she could by flailing her legs.

It's the rental boots and not my feet that smell, Ryuuji thought pointlessly as he bit his dry lips.

It was true that Taiga might not have needed him to take care of her anymore. Maybe he was just throwing a tantrum at the person trying to use all their strength to grow up and leave him behind.

It might have just been something as pathetic as that.

"Let! Me! Go!"

"..."

Just as Taiga leaned forward as far as she could, Ryuuji lifted his foot.

"AHHHHHHHHHH?! Don't just let goooooooooo!"

"Oh..."

It seemed that she had been kicking the snow harder than she thought. The sled suddenly took off, and Ryuuji panicked as he reached out to her but didn't make it. "I CAAAN'T STOOOP!" The tail end of her scream lengthened as she went straight down-hill—at least three meters.

"Aaaah!"

She bounced off a snow mound. Tragically, the sled leapt up and turned over, hurling Taiga forward. She dove face-first into the slope.

I told her so... Ryuuji groaned.

"I don't need your help! But it's your fault that I just fell!" Taiga, once again covered in snow, threatened him in a low voice. Ryuuji raised both his hands in the air. *I've got it. I won't make a move.*

But in that moment...

"Ngh?!"

Suddenly, Taiga was assaulted from the side by a terrific block of snow, and, once again, fell over from surprise onto the slope. As Ryuuji wondered what had happened...

"KYAA HA HA HA HA HA HA HA HA HA HA HA! AHA HA HA HA HA FWAH HA HA HA HA HA HA! HEE HA HA HA HA HA HA!"

The one who stood there, her mouth wide open and roaring with laughter like an ill-natured machine gun, and who had thrown the snow hard at Taiga, was Ami.

"Dimhuahua...why, you..."

"You're sooooo lame! Falling over on a sled is, like, miraculous! You're a miraculous idiot! Even I surrender! That's too pathetic! Actually, it's kind of impressive. KYA HA HA HA HA HA!"

Ami pointed at Taiga with her pole as she continued to roar with laughter. The look in Taiga's eyes rapidly changed, and her pupils started to widen. Her hair puffed up to the point one could see it rising.

"Kawashima, maybe you should run away?"

"I'm not so bad at skiing that this gremlin could follow me with a sled like that. ♥ Well, how about you try to follow me if you're mad? You'd probably be faster if you rolled down the slopes into a snowball like in a cartoon. BWAH HA HA HA!"

She began to calmly ski away.

"HMGH!"

Taiga's aim was accurate. The sled, which she had thrown, scored a direct hit on the back of Ami's head. Ryuuji shook as it happened right before his eyes. Without another word, Taiga charged at Ami where she had fallen.

"YAAAAAH!" She leapt on Ami, who was still fallen over on the slope.

"EEEEEK!" Ami's skis, which remained turned up, were splayed wide open.

"UGYAAAAAAAH!" Taiga held them down. She grabbed at Ami's gear and pulled hard at her limbs.

"Sh-she's being eaten alive..." Ryuuji covered his mouth and trembled as he watched.

"Ha ha ha ha!" Thoughtless and clearheaded, Kitamura skied right behind them. His teeth shone in a smile that looked like it could have come straight out of a commercial as he turned and lifted his goggles.

"What're you doing, Ami and Aisaka? No matter how open a snowy mountain feels, you can't do anything weird—NGAH!"

Ami had summoned the last of her strength to swing her pole, hitting Kitamura hard right in the crotch.

"Kushieda, Ami, and Haruta are on the top-level course. Noto, Kihara, Kashii, and I are on the mid-range course. Takasu and Aisaka are on the beginner's course."

At the words of the group leader Kitamura, who was walking slightly pigeon-toed, everyone politely answered, *Okay!*

As always, the weather was clear. In the strong afternoon sun, the slopes were much whiter, and they glittered blindingly. It was bright enough that it might have hurt their eyes if they didn't have goggles on.

For the afternoon, they would be divided up by level onto courses with coaches for the real ski practice. Everyone went up to the lift with each other but separated after that.

"Why don't you get some guts and follow them to the top course?"

"Why're you telling me that when you can't even do it... I'm fine with a sled, too."

Ryuuji and Taiga were whispering into each other's ears when they both sighed. According to what they had heard at noon, the beginner's course was that in name only. In actuality, only people who didn't have any skiing experience gathered there to play with sleds and make snowmen.

How's that fun on a school trip? Ryuuji thought, but it was also better than being forced to ski and getting hurt. If he forced himself to go to the top course just to be with Minori, everyone would be worried about him, and he would end up being a nuisance. He didn't want that. He couldn't even stand up. It wasn't as though Minori would support him from behind the whole time, either.

"Then we're going to the lifts! Everyone come this way! Make sure to have the lift ticket you were given around your neck!"

The other classes also started heading to the lifts, holding their skis. The diagram of primary colors wandered around. They were more or less a spectacle.

At that moment, Maya burst out in a quick tiptoeing run to follow Kitamura.

"Hey! Hey! Hey! Let's ride the lift together. I want to ride with you, Maruo!"

He had heard it... Ryuuji automatically turned to Taiga, who was a little behind him, but Taiga just gave an exaggerated shrug. They were going to ride lifts that were heading in a different direction. It wasn't as though she could do anything about it, he supposed.

"Oh yeah, that's fine, but you don't want to ride with Kashii?"

"I want to take a picture with Nanako while we're on the lifts, though! If we're on the same one, we couldn't get our whole bodies in, right? Right, Nanako?"

Her hair, which she had recolored to be slightly closer to black, was long and silky. Maya poked at her best friend, Nanako. Nanako giggled, her usual soft smile on her face.

"Yeah, that's true."

She communicated with Ami, next to her, with a look. Ami pouted her mouth in delight. The beautiful trio of girls had clearly already made a plan to snag Kitamura. Ryuuji glanced at Taiga's face, sure she was panicking.

"Taiga..."

"Huh?! Wh-what?! Get your face out of mine!"

What do you mean, what? He knit his eyebrows. There was something obviously strange about Taiga's behavior. Where in the world was she looking while her favorite, Kitamura, was being steadily led away by Maya? The moment their eyes met, she had jumped about five centimeters.

"Haven't you been acting kind of weird recently?"

"Recently? When? Actually, I feel normal. Normal, normal, normal. I'm normal."

There was definitely something strange going on. She wasn't acting normal, at least not when it came to Kitamura. Now that he thought of it, he had felt there was something off for a while. He felt like Taiga was being kind of strangely cold when it came to Kitamura.

Normally, Taiga would have made a huge deal about being in the same school trip group as Kitamura. Her face would have turned red as she said, "I want to be with Kitamura-kun!" In the end, it had worked out that way, but when it did, it felt like she was happier to be in Ryuuji and Minori's group, if anything.

"Like I said, what?! Don't stare at me like that!"

"..."

"I said don't look at me!"

No, he would look.

He thought about it. Maybe it was the opposite? He remembered the two of them talking at Taiga's condo. That was strange, too. If he had to describe it, it had felt like they shared a unique kind of solidarity in that moment, as though if one of them were to say, "About that thing we talked about earlier," the other would have known immediately what it was.

"Something happened with you and Kitamura, didn't it?"

"Huuh?! O-of course not! No no no! Nothing, nothing happened... Oh...maybe something did? Nothing happened, but I guess you could say something...maybe did? Yeah, I wonder if something happened? Uhh?"

Ryuuji was silent as, in front of his eyes, Taiga's face changed dizzyingly. Her face was practically a traffic light.

"D-did I not tell you? Right, something did happen. Umm, during the beginning of the year, I was walking around alone and happened to run into him. We went out to a café for a bit. That was it, that's all. Then we went on a shrine visit—uhh, what was it called again? Hatsumode? We did something like that."

"..."

Why didn't you tell me?

He didn't say it out loud. If he did, it would have made things feel awkward. But he still ended up thinking it.

Why didn't you tell me?

Oh, so that's why you two are all buddy-buddy now.

So, there was some kind of link between why she didn't tell him about meeting Kitamura and how she seemed somehow composed in her attitude toward him now. It wasn't so much that she was cool as just *composed.*

"Because back then, you were in the hospital! And then there was that other thing! It wasn't like I could be happy right then! I told you, right? I felt like I was to blame for it! So, so—huh?! Why am I explaining myself to you?! What is this?!"

"Why did you suddenly get angry?!"

Taiga's face rapidly blushed and turned rosy. She stomped on the snow, and her large eyes glittered.

"I don't have a duty to report every single thing that happens to me to you! I have things I can't tell anyone, too! Spilling my guts all the time would be weirder! I'm not gonna tell you anything I don't want to talk about! What's so wrong about that?!"

"It's not wrong or anything. Why're you getting mad for no reason?! There definitely is something weird going on with you! Either that, or you've got something really shady going on!"

Taiga made a shrieking noise. "GIIIII! L-L-Like I'd tell you everything, you idiot! There are a tooooooooon of things you'll never know in your lifetime! There are soooooooooooo many things I'd never tell you even if I were to die! Like I'd tell you!"

"Do whatever you want! If that's what you want, you can hide as many things as you want to! But I was telling you everything! If you don't want to tell me, then just take it with you to your grave! I don't care anymore!"

"I was going to do that without you telling me to! I don't care what you think, either!"

Taiga, now on the verge of tears, came at him with her sled. As their red and blue sleds clashed, Kitamura's voice echoed loudly behind them.

"Why are you two fighting?!"

Do you know what she did?! Ryuuji automatically turned around and—*BAM!*—was hit in the back of the head by Taiga's sled.

"You—you—you—!" He was assailed with a barrage of punches.

"Stop! Noto! Kihara!" Kitamura was yelling.

"Wait, they're not talking to us?!" Ryuuji slipped and fell.

"I don't care!" Taiga missed her last attack because he had fallen and self-destructed by burying herself in the snow.

Then, finally, they noticed. It seemed that they weren't the only ones having a fight.

"Why do you always butt in?! Why are you getting in the way?! You're so annoying, annoying, annoying, annoying! Annoooooooyiiiiiing!"

Maya was trying to hit Noto with her pole. Seeing people who normally never got angry making such a scene, Ryuuji and Taiga forgot what they had been doing.

"Eep, this is crazy..."

However, Noto hadn't lost yet. He grabbed his pole and pushed Maya back.

"Kihara, you're the one who's always acting selfish! You're always up to something, trying to hang around Kitamura! That's way more annoying!"

"I'm not up to anything! I'm not! I'm not! I'm not!"

"You were! You definitely were! You make everything convenient for yourself, that's how you always are, Kihara! Even right now!"

His glasses askew, Noto wailed as Maya attacked him again with her pole.

"Wh-what is this?!"

"Oh, did you finish? This just started." Casually keeping her distance from the scuffle, Nanako explained.

Maya had been planning to ride the lift with Kitamura, when Noto said something nasty, like, "Kihara's scheming something again." Maya got upset and replied, "It doesn't have anything to do with you, Noto." Then Noto said, "Show-offs stink." *Well, and the rest is what you can see now.*

"I wanted to say something a looooooong time ago, but Noto, all you do is get in my way! What's your problem?!"

"I'm not in your way! We just want our friend to be happy! Right, Haruta?! Isn't that right?!"

"Yes!" Haruta also joined the fray. He wrapped his arm around Noto's shoulder and stuck his tongue out at Maya.

"Sorry, but you guys' plan isn't working for us!" said Maya. "It's super shady, plus it's mind-numbingly boring!"

"What?!" said Noto. "I don't really care what happens to your mind when you're an idiot!"

"Ahhh, let's stop! I said stop! What's going on?!" Minori got between the three of them, trying to mediate. "Let's all get along! C'mon, we're on a school trip! Now, this is the end of your fight! Hand it over to me for safekeeping!"

Noto stubbornly pushed Minori back.

"What good's it gonna do if you get involved?! All you do is joke around, Kushieda! Sorry, but I'm gonna say what I want today! It's really, really gotten to me!"

"That's what I want to say!" said Maya.

Maya and Noto glared at each other with even darker expressions. Minori wailed, "I'm not messing around!" However, Noto and Maya weren't listening.

Kitamura, also looking troubled, quickly seized their poles. "I don't get what's going on!" he said. "How did this happen?! Anyway, let's cool down! Calm down!"

"Oh dear... We've got another idiot on our hands."

Kitamura turned around to look at his childhood friend, who had whispered that in a sugary-sweet voice. He couldn't hide his irritation. "You talking about me?"

"If you didn't know, then isn't it obvious? Ahh, I hate this. Hey, Yuusaku, are you so thick because you're oblivious? Or do you know what you're doing?"

"What are you trying to say?! Don't hint at it! Just say it!"

This time, it was Kitamura and Ami's turn. It might have been because they had known each other so long, but Kitamura's voice was three times louder and pricklier than usual as it echoed across the slopes. However, Ami's was more than five times pricklier.

"You want me to tell you exactly what it is?" she said. "You want me to tell it to you straight, but then you'll be all innocent, like, 'Oh, I had no clue!' And then you'll just be able to act surprised and not take any of the blame, because you're in the safe zone. That's such a nice position to be in. You're always like that, aren't you, Yuusaku? Even when we were kids."

"What?! What are you talking about?! How am I always in a safe zone?!"

"You're serious? You seriously don't know? You don't know why they're fighting?"

Exasperated, Ami faced the heavens. Kitamura looked back at her indignantly. *That's the type of guy Kitamura is*, Ryuuji thought. Noto and Haruta also exchanged knowing glances. That was the kind of guy Kitamura was. Why were the girls bringing it up now?

Nanako, who had stuck to not getting involved, whispered, "Ugh, is Maruo-kun seriously that oblivious? This is, like, violent..."

"Waaaaaah!" Maya started crying. Nanako and Ami ran to her and hugged her.

"Are you okay?! Don't cry, Maya!"

"Poor thing... Noto-kun, you're seriously horrible. I think you said too much. You should apologize to Maya."

"I should?! Why?! You think this was me?! You think it's me in the end?!"

Faced with Maya's crying, and Ami and Nanako's cold stares, Noto muttered, "I'm the one who wants to cry..." He didn't look cute at all, but he looked exactly like an otter. Without thinking, Ryuuji stepped towards Noto and patted him on the back. *Don't worry about it.*

"You're terwible, too, Takasu-kun! Waaaaaaah!"

"Am I the villain now?!"

Maya cried even harder, glaring at Ryuuji. "Weren'tweartners?! Weren'tweoneachothewr'ssides?! Then why? Whywouldn'tyoohewlpmeatahll?! Whyreyoosidingwihhim?! WAAAAAH!"

Weren't we partners?! Weren't we on each other's sides?! Then why? Why wouldn't you help me at all? Why are you siding with him? Waaaaah.

Perhaps because he had to decode what Yasuko was saying every day, Ryuuji understood what Maya was trying to say to him.

"L-Like I said! You fundamentally misunderstood!"

Ami, still holding the sobbing Maya's shoulder, glared at Ryuuji. Nanako glared at him, too. Taiga, being Taiga, turned her head away from him for a different reason as she snorted, "Hmph!"

The girls grouped up together, Minori and Taiga awkwardly sidling over to Ami and the rest. At least Minori didn't glare at him.

Ami seemed strangely satisfied as she nodded. "Now everyone!" Taking point as the girls' leader, she opened up her arms. "Let's get Maya to the bathroom! You guys are soooo terrible!"

Moving as one, with Maya in the middle, the girls left. Nanako turned around in the end and only had one thing to say.

"Ganging up on a girl to make her cry... You're the worst."

Watching the affair from a distance, people from other classes were shoulder to shoulder and passing their own commentary, delighted.

"What happened?!"

"Apparently it's a fight!"

"They made a girl cry!"

"What?!"

CHAPTER 4

The boys, who had been left behind, turned to each other and nodded.

We're not wrong at all.

We won't apologize to the girls.

Because we didn't do anything wrong.

Communicating through telepathy, they stuck their hands out and put them together. "Okay!"

When something like this happened, who cared about skiing? Staying together as a group? They cared even less about that. The four of them grabbed each other's hands, immediately got grossed out and let go, and then climbed onto the beginner's course lift.

It wasn't that they wanted to play on sleds or make snowmen. They wanted to talk about how they really felt without the girls being able to hear.

5

"**W**AIT A SECOND! You got in a fight with the girls?"

"You made Ami-chan and the other girls mad? What were you doing?!"

"Stuff happened. To sum it up, you're outta your mind if you think you can be friends with girls. They think they can make guys do whatever's convenient for them. They see us as their pawns. All they can think about is how to justify themselves for it. You'll never be able to be on an equal footing as friends." Noto pouted as he nibbled at his pickled vegetables.

"Well, that's probably enough," Kitamura admonished him.

Ryuuji washed down the last of his rice with miso soup and looked at the table where the five girls from their group had congregated. It looked like the situation was about the same over there—the girls were also talking to other people from Class 2-C.

Even with the heating, the dining room was sprawling and freezing. Filled with the groups of high school students, it bustled like a poked bee's nest under the fluorescent lamps. They'd finally been released from their terrible ski gear, free to wear tracksuits or their own clothes as they pleased, while they ate from the same menu.

Enjoying a good meal with everyone else should have been fun, but...

The girls had huddled together and were talking about something. They definitely had to be badmouthing the boys. Maya looked unhappy and sullen, and absolutely would not look at them. Looking a little troubled, but still trying to smile, Minori was talking brightly with Maya, but it seemed that she wasn't getting any results.

Under circumstances like these, Ryuuji couldn't ask how Minori actually felt, talk to her, or even approach her. It seemed like the trip might even end without him ever being able to. He hadn't even gotten in a fight with Minori, but given the situation, the other girls probably wouldn't let him talk to her.

Just how had they ended up in this boys-versus-girls scenario? Next to Minori, Taiga also looked troubled as she gripped her chopsticks and looked at a giant, dried-out, boiled fish. Normally, her gluttony couldn't even be subdued by a full serving of rice.

He and Taiga were both probably about as disappointed by how things had turned out. Ryuuji didn't think to question why Taiga would be upset—they had had a fight, after all. The back of his head still hurt from her hitting him with the sled. She had hit him over and over again, and he was just upset that he hadn't been able to get her back even once.

"Heey, Taka-chan, you wanna swap? Can I eat the rice you've got there?"

Ryuuji shook his head and gave Haruta the rest. Taiga wasn't the only one put off by the bland boiled fish. Regardless, Ryuuji still used his chopsticks to skillfully separate the meat from the bone so that it looked prettier.

"You don't have much of an appetite. You've just been poking at it and not actually eating anything."

Kitamura, who was sitting next to him, peeked at his hands. Ryuuji stopped.

"Hm? What is it?"

"No, nothing..."

Looking at Kitamura's face, Ryuuji wanted to put down his chopsticks. He'd just realized something.

It wasn't just Taiga who hadn't told him about going shrine visiting during New Year's—Kitamura hadn't, either. Now that he thought about it, the reason why Kitamura hadn't asked what happened to Taiga when she left the Christmas Eve party was probably because they met with each other behind Ryuuji's back.

Of course, Kitamura didn't need to tell him everything that had to do with Taiga! It was just a little strange that he hadn't said anything. It felt as though Taiga and Kitamura had colluded to keep something from him. What would he call this feeling? Was it alienation? Basically, was he just sulking?

There are things I don't tell you, Taiga had said to him. The world was still turning, even if he didn't know it. There were people living in places he had no clue existed, and they were doing as they pleased—why did it shock him to realize something so obvious as that now?

"You don't look too happy. In the afternoon...you and Aisaka had some sort of fight while we were out skiing. Is it that?"

"No...my stomach is upset. Sorry, I know it's dinner."

Even though he was super oblivious about his own stuff, Kitamura was strangely sharp when it came to how other people were feeling. In order to escape from that, Ryuuji stood up. He felt the presence of Kitamura's ever-watchful eyes on his back as he left the dining area alone.

Beyond the corridor with the cheap-feeling carpet that wasn't really to his taste, there was a dim lounge-like area that was a little worse for wear but had a bathroom in a corner.

Perhaps because it was cold, there weren't many people around. Ryuuji sat down on one of the sofas and breathed in. If someone asked him where he went, he wouldn't be lying if he said it was the bathroom.

Beyond the large window was the broad scenery of snow. The sky was already dark, but there were visitors going out night skiing, and the lights reflected off the slope.

At some point, powdery snow had started falling. It looked beautiful enough for him to want to take a picture, but he didn't really feel like doing it at that moment. Ryuuji closed his eyes.

"Ahhh..."

"I've caught a sigh!"

He practically jumped as he turned around.

Gotta catch 'em all! she said and gave him finger guns. Minori was standing there. Her black fleece jacket was zipped right up to her chin, and she was wearing casual cargo pants tied at the waist with a rope.

"You can't do that," she said. "Don't sit around sighing by yourself."

Her wide smile scrunched up her face as she turned to Ryuuji, who was so shocked he couldn't breathe.

"Why're you here...oh. The bathroom...sorry, I'll hang around over there instead so you can go in without worrying about me. Do your best."

He didn't know why he was doing it, but he gave Minori a fist pump, expecting her to go.

"Noooo! I saw you leave, Takasu-kun, so I told everyone I needed to go to the bathroom and left, too!"

"Huh..."

"Secrets should stay hush-hush, shush-shush."

Minori went around, putting a table between them as she sat down on a sofa. She looked him straight in the face. He could see her eyes light up. Ryuuji's heart felt like it was being squeezed.

What are you trying to say this time? he tried to say, but his mouth wouldn't move the way he wanted it to. What came out instead was "What say you...?" It made him sound like an old nobleman, but Minori seemed to get what he meant.

"Actually," she said, "I've been waiting for an opportunity for a while. Look, I have my hands full with Maya-chan still being like that, and you probably have to deal with Noto-kun, too. That was my thought process."

"Y-yeah..."

I was waiting for an opportunity, too! The thought felt like it was being squeezed out from the bottom of his gut. Ryuuji nodded his head up and down like a puppet. His neck felt stiff, and his whole body shook almost comically. He tried to move around so that Minori wouldn't notice and crossed his legs, but he couldn't stop trembling. He couldn't stop fidgeting, either.

He wanted a chance to ask Kushieda Minori how she really felt.

He wanted a chance to get a different answer.

Was this it? This might be it.

Trying to find words to say, he writhed as he faced her. However, Minori spoke first.

"This all turned into a fight, didn't it? I want to find a good way to settle it."

She looked serious, her forehead wrinkled. She hadn't even come close to broaching the subject about what was going on between them.

Gwah! Ryuuji choked on his own breath.

It's fine, he thought. *This isn't anything to get worked up about. Do it slowly. It's fine if it's slow.*

"H-how?"

"That's what I wanted to talk to you about. This school trip is supposed to be fun, after all. I really don't want it to end with everyone fighting. I want them to patch things up and go back to how we were."

"I do, too...right. That's what I was thinking, too."

I might even want the fight to end sooner than you. He didn't say that part out loud. Minori was scowling slightly as she nodded. She took her slippers off and put her hands on her folded knees as she sat with her feet ungraciously on the spongy sofa.

"I wonder if there's a good way to fix things? Basically, well, in the end...Maya-chan is all mixed up about Kitamura-kun, and that's the problem. That's one of the things that led to this."

"..." Ryuuji froze even further. His vital functions were going to stop, and he was going to turn to stone.

"So that's related... But actually, what happened was Noto-kun said some stuff that started the fight. And then everyone started saying the stuff they were already kind of thinking. Hmmm, this is going to be difficult..."

Minori hadn't even noticed that he'd turned to stone. As the dizziness closed in on him, Ryuuji thought, *How can you talk about people's love lives in front of the guy you rejected?*

"I wonder if you know, Takasu-kun?" Minori brought her defenseless, completely oblivious face even closer. "The reason why Noto-kun is trying to get in the way of Maya-chan's romance is because, well...he's got the wrong idea that Taiga-chan likes Kitamura-kun. Apparently, he's trying to cheer Taiga on, so he clashed with Maya-chan..."

Ryuuji knew he didn't have the right, but he couldn't help but feel something impatient and almost irritated rise up in him at her obliviousness. *What even is this?* he wanted to say. Just how little did she know? She was Taiga's best friend and didn't even know Taiga's feelings.

"Are you sure he's actually got the wrong idea?"

Ryuuji's voice was suddenly prickly. Minori's eyes went wide.

"There are things you don't know about Taiga, too, right Kushieda? Taiga might actually like Kitamura and just not have told you."

"There's no way... I try to know everything about Taiga."

You're saying that again... Ryuuji thought about telling her about Taiga and Kitamura going shrine visiting, but he just barely stopped himself. Spreading that around wouldn't help anyone. It was just an unshakable fact that Minori wasn't aware of.

Minori didn't know, and she didn't know she didn't know.

"Anyway," he said, "the situation is way more complicated than you think. But I agree with you about wanting to make everything better."

"It's complicated... You're right, it might be. It might be more complicated than either of us think. That might be true."

She pouted a little and pushed up her hair as though it were bothering her. The sound of the not-very-useful heater was the only thing that echoed through the lounge. Ryuuji was uneasily silent, and Minori was, too.

They definitely both had things they couldn't say to each other. Minori was acting as though she hadn't rejected Ryuuji. Ryuuji could tell that she didn't want to talk about it, but he didn't feel the same way. He couldn't forget what had happened. In fact, he wanted to try it again.

I used to be able to talk normally to her about things like this, he thought. So why couldn't he talk to her now?

"I wonder what we should do... Like really." Minori hummed in a low voice.

Realization dawned on Ryuuji at last. There was only one way to cancel out the discord between them, and that was for him to join her in pretending that she hadn't rejected him and that he hadn't been rejected by her. The two of them were like gears within the same mechanism that refused to bite and that resisted adjustment. They were starting to grate disharmoniously. If this kept up, the mechanism would break down.

If he wasn't able to follow along, pretending to be an oblivious part of Minori's nothing-happened-at-all world, their gears would never turn together.

But if he did, it would be nothing more than a lie.

Yes—that was right. Not a single thing had gone well so far. Not when they carried Taiga's bag together, not when they spoke window-to-window or were in Taiga's kitchen, not even when they were just skiing together. The reason why he had thought things were going well—the reason he'd thought they would be able to keep this up—was because he'd successfully deceived himself. It was because he'd stifled himself and gone along with Minori.

If Ryuuji ever tried to change Minori's path, he would lose his balance. Just like when they were skiing.

"Hmm, we need to do something for the sake of the trip. Plus, this is the last one. I'd really hate that... I really want us to just stay like this." Minori slowly put her hand in her pocket and pulled out something small and shiny. She used it to pin up her pesky bangs.

"Where'd you get that?"

"Hm? This hairpin? Taiga gave it to me. She told me it's special, so I have to keep it really, really safe or something. Cute, huh? Oh, I don't mean me, I mean the pin."

As Minori smiled, an orange hairpin glittered in her hair. It was the one Ryuuji had chosen himself. So Taiga had had it all along.

"Ha ha..."

Ryuuji laughed and put his face in his hands.

I'm done.

After seeing the hairpin that had been the last remnant of his feelings for Minori, he realized that the gears had broken beyond repair. If you tried to forcibly align things that just wouldn't work together—well, look. Everything would come crashing down.

She wanted things to stay as they were. She didn't want anything to change. Minori had said as much herself. *It would be better if everyone could stay like this. It would be better if we could always be like this.*

To turn in harmony with Minori's gear, Ryuuji would have to take that hairpin and stomp on it in secret to kill the truth. He would have to kill a part of himself.

He could have gone along with Minori's nothing-ever-happened world, laughed it off, and pretended he hadn't ever been rejected. But...he couldn't do that anymore. Ryuuji's heart was still alive. If he tried to kill it, he'd just be bleeding.

Everything that had played out so far was all a way for Minori to create proof that nothing had happened. The feeling of when she had touched him, when they laughed and he felt ticklish, even her coming out of her way now to see him—all of it.

She was doing it all on purpose. So she could pretend Christmas Eve had never happened.

"Aha ha...right... so that's how it was."

"What's wrong, Takasu-kun? Why have you been so quiet? What is it? Hey?"

"No! It doesn't matter anymore."

Ryuuji kept his face covered but opened his eyes.

Everything was in pieces. He couldn't stand bleeding in secret or deceiving himself any longer. Minori's desire to keep the status quo basically meant Ryuuji would have to keep slaying his feelings, and Minori knew that. She'd gone out of her way to preemptively reject him that night on Christmas Eve because she knew that, and still, she wished for nothing to change.

I'm stubborn and unfair, Minori had said to him in the past. He finally understood what she meant.

If you like me, stubborn and unfair as I am, then you need to still like me despite knowing that. She wanted him to be aware of that, even as she asked him to crush his own heart. She wouldn't reciprocate, but if that was fine with him, he could keep on liking her.

But why?

Why wouldn't she just tell him that she didn't want to date him because she didn't like him?

Oh, I see. It's because she's stubborn and unfair.

It was because she didn't have the courage to hurt him.

"Takasu-kun...Takasu-kun! What's wrong? Did something happen? Sorry...did I say something wrong?"

Ryuuji raised his head and smiled as though to say, *Nothing, nothing's wrong. There's nothing wrong at all.* He stood up and took two large steps away from Minori. When he heard her voice call to him, "Where are you going?" he turned on his heel without saying a word.

Everyone was probably still in the dining hall. He kept his smile plastered on his face as he quickly walked down the hallway and back to the bustling dinner area. He went back to the table, where only his seat remained empty.

"I'm going to go back to the room early. My stomach hurts. Where are the keys?"

"Takasu..."

He realized Kitamura was shocked at the sight of his face. He realized that Noto and Haruta had stopped talking and were looking at him, too.

But they said nothing, and Ryuuji took the keys and left the dining area.

Ryuuji had thought the worst night of his life was Christmas Eve. He couldn't have imagined that those ugly memories would be unearthed so soon.

He returned to the dim and dusty smelling Japanese-style room on his own and quickly laid out one set of the bedding that had been piled in a nook. He set his bed up in the farthest corner of the room possible. He didn't even tuck in the sheets but only put out the bottom-most layer of bedding and threw the pillow and blanket down onto it. He hadn't even taken his evening bath, and he was still in a sweatshirt and sweatpants, but he dove right in.

He wanted an hour—no, even just thirty minutes alone like this. He prayed no one would come into the room.

On *that* night, he'd had a home to return to. There was a bed he could slip into without anyone seeing. On top of that, his flu symptoms had started, and his head had been fuzzy. Even his memories of going home were ambiguous, like it had been a dream.

Now, though, reality was playing out incredibly clearly and tangibly before his own eyes. It was being etched right into the folds of his brain.

Kushieda Minori would never accept his feelings. Kushieda Minori had decided that. It was a reality he couldn't change. She had scrubbed everything clean from start to finish so that Ryuuji's unrequited love no longer even existed.

Minori would never accept that he liked her. She wouldn't even accept that his feelings existed in this world. *Ghosts aren't real, UFOs are just your eyes playing tricks on you, and Takasu-kun doesn't have feelings for me.*

That's how it was.

But why?

Why?

He held his pillow, rounded his body up, and squeezed his eyes shut. He bit his lip. *Please, please, make it so no one comes into this room.*

At that moment, he heard shuffling.

"Takasu, what's wrong? Did something happen?"

"Is he asleep? We're worried about you, Takasu. We're just worried."

"Does your stomach actually hurt? Did you eat something by yourself?"

His wishes were easily betrayed. The three guys gathered around him without hesitation.

You've got to be kidding—unfortunately this was reality, too.

Pretending he hadn't heard anything, Ryuuji stayed curled up in the bedding like a raccoon.

"Hey, you." Haruta's finger poked him right in the butt. If he really had been sleeping because his stomach hurt, that would have spelled disaster. "What? He's seriously sleeping?"

Haruta actually tried to pull the covers off him. Ryuuji held onto them, but resisting too much would have been suspicious, and he was forced to let go. The covers were stripped right off of him, and Ryuuji felt the creepy sensation of the idiot's breath on his cheek as Haruta looked over his face. He curled up his whole body and desperately kept his eyes closed.

"Ugh..."

"Oh, there we go! Let's see, is he really sleeping?"

He absolutely didn't have it in him to tell everyone what had happened. He just wanted to be alone right then. He wanted them to somehow read his *leave-me-alone* aura.

"Aw, he's asleep. Ah well. Then we'll just have to be really quiet!"

Right, right, that was good. *Sorry, Haruta. Sorry, everyone.* But the moment Ryuuji began to feel the slightest bit of relief, the most mind-boggling of comments came from none other than Noto's mouth.

"Hey, Kitamura, what do you think you're doing?! Why're you taking off your clothes all of a sudden?!"

The eyelids of the sleeping raccoon twitched. *Stop. Don't do that.* Ryuuji held his breath in spite of himself, feeling some incredibly unpleasant presence nearby.

"Well, Takasu is sleeping, so I thought I'd get ready for bed, too."

"Gaaaah! Why're you taking off just your pants? How perverted are you, master—I mean, ass-ter?!"

"I'm sleeping with my shirt on. Now, where's my bag? Where'd it go?"

"Ahhhhhh! You're being a little too liberal, ass-ter!"

"Put that thing back! This is too realistic!"

Kitamura...your bag is on the bottom shelf of the cupboard! Ryuuji desperately told him, but unfortunately, it seemed his telepathy didn't reach Kitamura. He heard Kitamura walking on the tatami mats. Just imagining Kitamura's disrobed state was terrifying, and even more terrifyingly, those footsteps came to a halt directly above Ryuuji's pillow. They stopped literally right above his head.

He can't be straddling my head right now. His mind was occupied by the unthinkable image—

"Oh, dear. I feel some mysterious gassy substance coming out of my butt..."

"That's a direct hit, Kitamura! It's not even going to filter through anything!"

"Phew! You're the worst! Poor Taka-chan, that's such a tragic fate!"

No way.

No way. No way. No way. Nowaynonononono—

"Poot."

"YOU...IDIOOOOOOOOOOT!"

Ryuuji sat up.

"Kitamura, you better not have gotten your noxious, filthy spray of E. coli-filled gas on my face—oh?!"

"We lied..."

"I didn't think he'd believe it..."

"He so fell for it..."

He faced the three stooges. Kitamura stood over Ryuuji, fully clothed in his normal tracksuit, hands pressed together as he squeezed the air between them out into jovial "Poot poot poot ♪" noises.

"Why...you..."

For a good five seconds, Ryuuji just looked at them in a stupor.

"ARGH! Do you guys even know how terrified I was?!"

"Sorry, but we were worried because you were acting weird."

Faced by Kitamura's serious face, Ryuuji held his head and writhed. He couldn't put it into words, but he wanted to tell them, *You're the ones being weird with that convincing performance!*

"So, what happened?" Noto also looked earnestly at Ryuuji with eyes about half the size of Kitamura's (and they weren't cute).

Haruta said, "My feet are cold. Lemme under there, too." He tried to force his toes into the toasty covers Ryuuji was under.

"Nothing...really...happened..."

"Would a guy who had nothing happen to him go back to the room on his own and pretend to sleep? You were worried about me before, and you talked to me about it. This time, I—we—want to do that. If there's anything we can do, we want to do it. We're worried about you. Talk to us, please."

Kitamura sat down with his legs folded directly under him and leaned forward. Ryuuji understood painfully well the feelings that made Kitamura say that. He really had been worried the time Kitamura had gone blond.

But Kitamura has things he can't talk about himself, doesn't he? Ryuuji ended up thinking.

"Hey...please."

Suddenly, he felt embarrassed for thinking that. The moment he raised his eyes, he was hit with Kitamura's sincere, direct gaze. Noto and Haruta were looking straight at Ryuuji's eyes, too.

These guys were his friends.

Whether he liked it or not, they were allies.

All allies did was believe in the person they were there for, didn't they? If an ally didn't tell him something, then Ryuuji just had to believe they'd had a reason for it. It was time to throw up his hands.

Ryuuji—mostly unconsciously—had already raised his hands in unconditional surrender.

"I couldn't tell any of you for a long time, but..." He hesitated. "I-I..."

Haruta straightened up. Noto and Kitamura had already been sitting upright.

"...l-l-l-liked Kushieda, but—"

"Wha?!"

"Huh!"

"Keep going!"

"...she rejected me on Christmas Eve..."

"Ngh..."

"Uhh!"

"Keep going!"

"...then I talked to her just now...and it's completely over..."

"Guh..."

"Fwoo..."

"K-keep going!"

"That's all I've got!"

Whoo! Ryuuji collapsed. All the strength rushed out of him at once, and the inside of his head went white. He felt like he was about to crumble into ash. He felt like he'd be scattered by a passing wind.

All of them were silent.

Kitamura looked stealthily at Noto. Noto was looking hesitantly at Haruta. Then Haruta looked slowly into Ryuuji's eyes.

....

"WAAAAAAAAAAAAAAAAAAAAAAAAAAAAAAAAAAH!"

They flipped.

"EEEEEEEEK!" "WAAAAAAAAH!" "OHHHHHHHH!" They yelled like idiots. "NUOOO!" They writhed, rolled on the ground, scratched at the floor, and arched their bodies backward.

"What the hell, Takasu?! Since when?! Kushieda... Kushieda! KUSHIEDAAAAA?!"

"Wait, Takasu, why? Why is that how it is, and how is it like that, like why?!"

"Kushieda?! Kushieda?! Huh, but Kushieda... You can't possibly mean *that* Kushieda?!"

Ryuuji jutted out his chin and stared at the ceiling. "That's right! It's Kushieda Minori! That—that weird girl is the one I liked for over a year! I'm sorry I ever liked her! But she doesn't seem to have feelings at all! It's like she couldn't even imagine it happening! She doesn't feel anything for me, I'm telling you! Nothing at all! WHYYYYYY?!"

He fell face down onto the blankets. He didn't care what happened anymore. He didn't even care if he breathed in mites. He didn't even care if he had a slight allergic reaction. He wouldn't even care if he started crying right there.

"But actually, come to think of it, you and Miss Kushieda were pretty close, weren't you?! Like I remember seeing you guys talking enough to make me think twice?!"

At Noto's voice, good old Haruta with his weak memory followed suit.

"I thought so, too!"

Like that would console him... Ryuuji started to deny it, but they kept going.

"Why'd Miss Kushieda reject you, Takasu?! What's her reasoning?! I can't accept that—like at all! I haven't heard of her having a boyfriend either, and it's not like she'd like anybody else?! But I'd never ever have imagined...a guy liking Kushieda! Like seriously, why?!"

"That's what I want to know! Why don't you ask her?" Ryuuji wailed desperately.

"How about we do it? Let's ask her."

Kitamura quickly stood up. *Huh?* Ryuuji looked up at his face.

"I can't believe it either. If I'd been a girl, I definitely would've dated Takasu."

Me, too! Yup, yup! Noto and Haruta raised their voices. Kitamura's expression was completely serious. He pushed his glasses up on his nose as he declared this without hesitation.

"Are you an idiot?!" said Ryuuji. "That's not funny! That's not even a joke!"

"Well, it's not just asking Kushieda about you, Takasu. Actually, I'm in the mood to ask the girls some stuff."

"Then why don't you pay a visit to their room by yourself?! D-D-D-Don't use me as an excuse!"

Kitamura put a gentle hand on Ryuuji's shoulder as he writhed.

"Instead of staying in bed like this, you should be facing up against the girls, fair and square, starting with Kushieda. There's been so much happening today, even my head feels like it's going to explode. Since it's come to this, we might as well be frank about it. Nothing comes of fighting! Mutual understanding is the first step to a stable society!"

"No, no, no! There's something wrong with what you're saying! Don't get me involved, I'm begging you!" Ryuuji waved his hands in a desperate attempt to stop Kitamura's recklessness.

"Well, Takasu, there's stuff I want to ask the girls, too. So, let's go. I'm pretty sure the girls' room is one floor down."

"Taka-chan! This is definitely how you get your revenge! Like no matter what happens...we want to protect our precious Taka-chan! I won't forgive her for rejecting you! Curse you, Kushieda!"

"Okay, let's go. Right now."

"Okay, we're all going now. C'mon Takasu."

"HURAH! GURAH! We're coming for you, Kushieda!"

"Stop, stop, stop! Stop! Anyway, just sit down—huh?!" Ryuuji grabbed Kitamura's enthusiastic arm and tried to stop him, but instead, his hand was taken, and he was pulled right out of bed.

"Noto, you have the key, right?! Let's go!"

"Wait, wait, wait, you're serious?! You're really serious?!"

The other three nodded solemnly.

"This is just like Chushingura—that story where the forty-seven ronin avenge their master. If you're the master, Asano Naganori, then we're the Aka-roshi that were involved in the attack."

"Aren't you just using me as an excuse to go there?!"

"Think of Kushieda as the villain in Chushingura—she's Kira. But we're trying to have a gentlemanly conversation with her. Okay, room's locked."

"It's not like we can talk to them about it! We'll just end up getting in another fight!"

"Oh yeah, Kira. He's so cool! I've got every volume! It's kind of hard to follow though! Maybe I'll cut my hair, too! Bringing a manga to the hairstylist might be kind of embarrassing, though?!"

"I think you're talking about something completely different? Whoa!"

Kitamura and Noto took off running down the hall, and Haruta followed after them without hesitation.

"Hey! Damn it...seriously...seriously. I seriously don't care what happens anymore!"

Ryuuji was on the verge of crying, but he couldn't stand them pulling a Chushingura without him. He ran after his friends as fast as he could.

"We're coming in, girls! Be good now and open this door... Wait, it's already open?!" The door just popped open as Kitamura grabbed the cheap-looking doorknob.

"We got hella lucky! Hey, gals! I don't know if you're changing or doing something else, but you're the exhibitionists for not locking up!"

"We're heading in, Kitamura, Takasu!"

Haruta opened the door without hesitation and dove in. He pushed Kitamura before him and grabbed Ryuuji's arm. Noto followed after them. As they rushed into the room, Ryuuji froze up, automatically preparing himself for shrieks and denunciations.

"Huh? What? No one's here!"

"Yeah...they're just careless. Actually, what even is this?!"

Ryuuji looked around the eight-tatami mat room and scowled like a medium possessed by a spirit. Could this room really have the exact same layout as theirs?

The girls' five people's worth of bags were laid out right on the floor. The ones that had their zippers closed were in a better state, but there were several that were wide open, their contents spilling out. Brushes, hot curlers, phones with too many key chains on them, pouches, magazines, and girly stuff that he didn't recognize were scattered all around. They had dropped their still-damp gear wherever they wanted, and the only things they'd put up on hangers were two jackets and four skirts.

To top it all off, there was just a single sock thrown into a corner. Ryuuji really just could not stand socks in uneven numbers.

"This is so gross! Ahhh!"

"Hold back, Takasu! You can't clean this!"

As Kitamura held him back, Ryuuji's body shook. Incidentally, under Ryuuji's instructions, the boys had put all their bags into the cupboard and put their uniforms up on hangers. Their gear was already wiped down and drying by the window. He even had a rule that everyone had to put their personal belongings back in their bags after using them.

These eight-tatami mat rooms had to have four to five high school students stuffed into them, after all. If they didn't clean it up right, they wouldn't be able to keep their own zones of privacy. Plus, messes always invited friends. If one thing was left out, it would immediately contaminate the area around it. If a place was messy, the minds of those living in it would also be scattered. Actually, if he had to live in such a small, messy, chaotic room like this, Ryuuji would probably have gotten sick.

How did they even do that...? Why wouldn't they want to live in more comfort for the two nights and three days they would be there? He at least wanted to do something immediately about that gear and those uniforms. The gear would get smelly, and the pleats of the skirts would get all messed up...

No. He couldn't. Ryuuji bit his lip and desperately turned his eyes away from the area he wanted to clean.

"They left the room unlocked when it's like this... I wonder if they thought it'd lock automatically behind them? Maybe they're at the baths? Just how many snacks did they bring?" Noto also seemed exasperated as he looked around the room. Then, he exclaimed, "Oh!"

"What's wrong, Noto-chi?"

"I saw it! I saw a camisole! It's blue!"

"I found a whole bunch of damp towels! Whoo!"

Haruta raised the treasures he had found. Class 2-C's conscience, Kitamura, admonished them. "Hey, stop that you two! And even you? Takasu, stop!"

"Oh no...I'm not doing that. That's not what I meant." Ryuuji quickly hid that unbearable, single dropped sock behind his back.

"Seriously, even you, Takasu? You can't touch other people's personal stuff. Now, put it back! Oh no, I stepped on something. What is this... 'Aroma cream'? Oh...so it's a type of hand cream, and you can put it on your face? Ohhh...yeah, that's an aroma. It smells like what you'd imagine for an aroma."

"Lemme see, oh..."

"Yeah, this is it. It's an aroma..."

"Ohh...it's kind of a sexy smell, hee hee."

Kitamura had squeezed a tiny bit of the cream from the tube onto the back of his hand, where everyone sniffed it. Kitamura rubbed it in and said, "Yeah, it's smooth." How was this the conscience of class 2-C?

"Hee hee..."

Suddenly Haruta laughed.

"If anyone were looking at this scene right now, we'd really look like perverts. This is the kind of thing you end up in cuffs for."

"Stop being stupid. We just came here for revenge, right? Our final goal was to be diehards."

That was right. Ryuuji and Kitamura nodded at Noto's words.

"But we look kind of outrageous."

Well, they might have looked weird from an outside perspective.

Haruta had a towel someone else had used around his neck. Noto still had the camisole in his hands. Ryuuji was still hiding the sock. And Kitamura was being allured by the fragrance of the cream he'd rubbed on his hand.

"You're right that it might look like that," Kitamura said. "We might look a little dangerous, but we're not perverts, and we didn't come here aiming to mess with the girls' stuff. How about we put everything back before the girls come in, and then start over, my friends?"

It was a splendid idea. Everyone agreed, but just then...

Clack. The door the perverts had come in through to mess with the girls' personal things began to open.

Out of anyone it could have been, it was Taiga.

The boys just barely managed to jump into the small closet, their hearts racing. Out of all the girls, the most savage and unreasonable one had come back to the room alone.

They lined their eyes up to the slightly open sliding door, where a line of light spilled through, to see the room.

"This is bad. This is bad..."

Shhhh. They hushed Haruta's wail, but Ryuuji, too, felt overwhelmed with despair and was close to peeing himself. This went two steps beyond just playing around with people's personal belongings while the owners weren't present. They couldn't say, "We're diehards" or "We're getting revenge," anymore. There was absolutely no way they could say any of that now.

Still unaware of the fact Ryuuji and the rest were watching from their hiding place, Taiga threw her key onto the tatami. It looked like she hadn't even noticed that the door had been open.

She'd probably just finished taking a bath. She was wearing a parka and, unusually for her, matching pants. Her long hair was still soaking wet. Her face was red, and she was breathing loudly.

Taiga wiped her hair with the towel around her shoulders and grabbed a dryer that she had left sitting right out in the middle of the room. She pulled on the cord as she let her eyes wander around. It seemed she was looking for an outlet. There was one right before her eyes in an easy-to-spot location, but Taiga seemed despondent.

"Guess there isn't one..." she muttered, and her shoulders slumped.

Ryuuji slipped. If his butt hadn't fallen onto Noto's leg, he probably would have made a sound.

"Takasu!"

"Sorry!"

Ryuuji couldn't help it—Taiga was just too much of an idiot. She hadn't even noticed the outlet right in front of her! She gave up on the dryer, tossed it aside, and then trotted across the room as though she'd remembered something. She opened the room's refrigerator and pulled out a bottle of tea she seemed to have brought with her. Perhaps she was feeling thirsty from her bath. Taiga put a hand on her hip and heartily tipped the tea back.

"Gah-hah!"

She coughed hard, and in that moment, spilled tea all over the place. "Oh, ew."

Don't say ew... Inside the closet, the same sentiment bloomed like a cloud. Ryuuji felt like grinding his teeth as he looked at the tea spilled on the ground. If they didn't wipe it up quick, it'd form a stain.

As though Ryuuji's thought had made its way to her, Taiga immediately bent down and started wiping the tea off the tatami.

But—she used the towel she had been using on her hair. What was she going to do with her wet head now?

As Ryuuji watched, disturbed, Taiga did the unthinkable. With that very same towel, she once again started drying her hair.

Whaaaaa?! Even Haruta made a low noise. Ryuuji nearly fainted. *Oh, Taiga—why are you so careless?*

Despite that, when Taiga started drinking her tea again a bit more carefully, her profile really looked exactly like a doll. She looked like a princess from a fairy tale.

"Guff!"

Stop... Don't burp either, please.

Taiga capped the bottle and held it in one hand as she started wandering around the room. She wiped her hair with the tea towel as she walked.

"Ah!"

She tripped on someone's bag. *BAM!* She fell onto her face. And then, out of all the things that could have happened...

"Ow!"

...the bottle that had flown out of her hand landed right back down onto her head.

"...!"

"Oh..." The boys wriggled, covering their mouths before they could blurt anything out. The klutz god had descended to earth right in front of them. That said, this was probably an everyday occurrence for Taiga.

"Ugh, what's with this...ngh..."

Taiga held her head but stayed calm. Still on the ground, she rolled over onto her back and lay splayed out on the tatami. She yawned. She arched, and her back cracked loudly. Then she closed her eyes and began to hum.

Vrmmmm vrmmm. ♪ Vrmmmmm vrmmmm. ♪

Her humming sounded just like a mass of cicadas. That was Ryuuji's limit.

"Bwah ha!"

"Huh?!"

Within the closet, three fists hit Ryuuji in the back. However, the sound he'd released could no longer be taken back. With her usual cat-like reflexes, Taiga leapt up. She held her bottle like a bat.

Her pale face looked like a Noh mask, and her large, emotionless eyes were open so wide they seemed like they might split at the seams. Taiga scanned the whole room and somehow, now of all times, came to the correct conclusion. She stared at the closet.

Bottle held high in her right hand, and poised to defend her face with her left, her footwork was obviously far from amateur as she stepped towards the closet.

And then, something unthinkable happened.

What if Tiger locked the room and went to sleep?

Unbelievable! But when it comes to Tiger, I'd believe it.

Aha ha ha ha...

They heard the sound of four people laughing. They heard Maya and Ami's voices approaching them through the thin walls of the closet. They were close. They were almost there.

And then, right before them, Taiga's hand was on the sliding door.

"Ahh! To hell with it!"

It was his fault for making a noise. Ryuuji sent up a quick prayer to heaven and then, faster than Taiga could reach out her hand, he suddenly threw open the sliding door. *BAM!*

"Eeeeeeeeeeeeeep..."

It seemed that when people were truly afraid, they couldn't even scream. Taiga made a noise like a strangled baby monkey as Ryuuji appeared before her eyes and grabbed her legs, making her fall backward onto her butt.

"Please, please, be quiet, please! Sorry, sorry, sorry, sorry, please, forgive us!"

"HAGBHAABABABARYURYURYU..."

Ryuuji grabbed her frozen arm and pulled her into the bottom half of the closet while apologizing, his face in full-on possessed-medium mode. Taiga was halfway to fainting.

"I'll explain things later," he said, as if he were a husband caught cheating. The timing was dangerous and last minute.

"Huh, it's still open. Hey, Tiger, you're so careless!"

The door opened with a clack, and Maya's voice echoed through the room... Just as Kitamura quietly closed the sliding door.

"Hel...!"

...lp me! Taiga probably tried to yell.

"Please...just this once...please...please, okay..."

Ryuuji had become an actual pervert. He whispered hotly into Taiga's ear as he begged her, pinning her arms behind her back with all the strength he could muster. He could feel the warmth from her skin through her parka and pants, as though she were a child who had just come out from the bath.

This really could land him in jail. On top of that, even as he apologized, he covered her mouth. Taiga tried to bite him like a wild animal, but he somehow stopped her from screaming. Her wet hair flailed, and her hard head hit his chin. *BAM!*

Even then, Ryuuji didn't yell. He couldn't make the same mistake again. He noticed the thinness of the arm he held so tightly, and weakened his grip, but then she butted his chin again hard enough to make him feel like he might die. Her strength weirdly reassured him. He felt something that was a little different from guilt, but it dispersed with his pain.

"Huh? Taiga's not here...but she said she'd come back first to dry her hair."

"The key is over there, so maybe she went to the bathroom? Ahh, that was a nice bath. It wasn't a hot spring, but it's nice when it's that big."

"I so agree. I want to go in again later. We can go as many times as we want before lights out, right?"

"Nanako, you seriously love baths. But if you're going, I'll go, too. I want to get thinner. Actually, Ami-chan, why don't you become a pinup model? I think you'd seriously be a hit! For sure!"

"You think so? It's not like I want to become an entertainer, though."

As soon as they entered the room, Minori, Ami, Maya, and Nanako immediately started talking. They were bustling around, asking to be handed their toner, eating snacks, and turning on the TV. No one had noticed the secret sexual harassment feud in the closet, but Ryuuji couldn't hold back the Palmtop Tiger all by himself forever.

Just when he thought it was only a matter of time before Taiga escaped, Maya spoke.

"Hey... Maybe Tiger went to the boys' room by herself? Maybe she's with Maruo-kun right now."

Maya wrapped her long hair with a towel and plopped down cross-legged. Taiga's body froze as her name was said. Kitamura probably jolted, too.

Across from Maya, Nanako smiled, putting cream on her face (the same one Kitamura had been rubbing on his hand). She sat down, as well.

"Tiger? Go to the boys' room by herself? No way. You're overthinking it."

"Oh, but maybe she's doing *something* with Takasu-kun, and Yuusaku will come by, and there'll be a situation," Ami said. "That could happen."

"What do you mean, they're doing 'something'?" Nanako poked fun back at Ami. Ryuuji agreed with Nanako, too. *What are we supposedly doing?* he thought.

"What?! It'd be so terrible if that actually did happen! Actually...what is it with Tiger, really? Is she actually after Maruo? No matter what anyone says, the one she's really the closest to is Takasu-kun, isn't it? Back when we went to Tiger's house, Takasu-kun was doing the dishes. That's pretty clear, isn't it? Maybe the whole Maruo thing is just a misunderstanding, and in the end, she's really after Takasu-kun? Honestly, that'd be nice!"

That was the point at which Taiga stopped resisting. Even if she got free of Ryuuji's arms, this newest development put Taiga in a situation where she couldn't really jump out and say, "I've been here the whole time!"

She stopped moving and looked up for a second at Ryuuji's face. He felt like her lips were moving to mouth something. *Remember this...*

"Hey, Kushieda, what's going on with that? You're close to Tiger, right? Who is Tiger really after, Takasu-kun or Maruo? It's Takasu-kun, right? Right?"

"Well, that's hard for me to say, partner. Why don't you ask Taiga directly when she gets back?" Pinning up her washed hair with a clip, Minori cocked her head.

"What?! It's not like Tiger would tell us! Actually, Kushieda, you've been kind of quiet since earlier? What happened?"

"You think so? I might have skied too hard. I'm kind of sleepy."

"What?! We're not going to let you sleep tonight! We're having girl talk! Actually, if Tiger would just like, hurry up and get Takasu-kun already, we wouldn't have any problems!"

"Oh, that stings...and then Minori-chan pleads the fifth. ♥" Ami smiled suggestively.

For a moment, the air in the room froze. The air in the closet froze in the same way.

"Huh, what? What do you mean? Ami-chan, I wanna know. You do, too, right, Nanako?"

"Yeah, of course. Actually, Ami-chan said something that only Kushieda got a while ago, too, right?"

"Ohh, you two heard that? Sorry, Minori-chan...you pretend to be oblivious so often that I've said too much, now."

Minori turned to face Ami. Ami was blinking her big Chihuahua eyes, acting purposefully cute as she smiled and looked back at Minori.

"Look, don't just talk to each other through your eyes. Just say it, Ami-chan!"

"Maya's asking, but should I say it? Should I let it out?"

Minori tilted her head. "Say what?"

Ryuuji swallowed. Putting aside the dangerous topic at hand, it was Minori's expression that got to him. Her eyes were a little narrowed, and her chin was raised. She was looking right through Ami.

He'd seen that face once before. He could never forget it. It was during the practice for the culture festival. Minori had asked him about Taiga's dad, and her face now looked exactly the same as it had back then.

In other words, it was her face when she was actually angry.

But Ami wasn't cowed. She put a placid smile on her face. Then she said:

"Minori-chan rejected Takasu-kun when he tried to confess to her on Christmas Eve. Did you forget? No way, that's how precious popular girls are! You're so calm about it! How cool! Like you don't even remember that you rejected him! Aha ha!"

"Huh? What? Whaat?! Takasu-kun tried to confess to you?! Seriously?!"

"And then you rejected him?! On Christmas Eve?! No waay! Actually...how do you know that, Ami-chan?!"

"I wonder... It's a mystery."

Maya and Nanako were getting excited, but next to them, Minori inhaled and said, indifferently, "Ahmin...I wonder why you would say that..."

Ami replied, "Because you were acting so airheaded all the time. I can't believe you're pretending everything is fine."

Her words and voice were terrifyingly true to her nature. She came directly at Minori, targeting her weaknesses, spoiling for a fight.

"Takasu-kun likes Minori-chan, not Tiger, it turns out. But, Minori-chan rejected him. But now she's acting all oblivious, like, 'We all need to get along!' and 'Don't you wanna be like this forever?' Like...what? Do you really think someone can stay friends with the girl who rejected him? You were obviously clinging to him on purpose when we were skiing. You were just trying to show him how oblivious you are, right? Just how cruel are you?"

The team in the closet and the one in the room both swallowed without thinking. No one could say a word...

"When did you see me acting fine? Did you really see that? What do you know about me? Can your eyes see through to my heart? Actually, this doesn't have anything to do with you, Ahmin. Don't stick your nose into this."

...other than Minori, that was.

"So this doesn't involve me, huh? Oh, I see. Sorry. But...when I heard that you rejected Takasu-kun, I had this thought that you might be acting out of a sense of guilt. I guess it doesn't involve that..."

"I told you already. It has nothing to do with you. I don't know what you're trying to say. If you think I'm doing fine, then that's great. Just leave it alone."

"Oh, good. I'm so relieved it doesn't have anything to do with me. And that it doesn't have anything to do with the *guilt,* either. Oh, what a relief—so Minori-chan and Takasu-kun clearly aren't as upset as I thought. See, I thought you'd rejected Takasu-kun because of guilt over a *certain* someone, Minori-chan, but I guess you just really genuinely hate him? I'll tell Takasu-kun that tomorrow. I'll tell him you rejected him because you hate him. It's much kinder not to string him along, like you are now. You should just tell him exactly what you think and break things off."

"Do what you want..."

"Okay, I get the message. Oh, maybe I'll go tell him right now?"

"I said you could do what you want."

"Your face looks pretty great on the surface..."

"What're you even saying?"

"I wonder what I mean..."

"Get a hold of yourselves!" Maya sounded resolute as she intervened. Time, which seemed to have frozen over, finally started to creak forward again.

"Ami-chan, what's gotten into you, too? Let's stop. We're on a nice school trip and fighting among girls is just so—I don't want to know any more about this! It's Noto we should be angry at! Isn't that enough? Kushieda, you too, okay? Let's just move on from this, please!"

"I think it'd be really hard on Tiger if she came back and she saw you two still fighting," Nanako said. "Tiger's parents are divorced, aren't they? I only have one parent at home, so I get it. When you see your friends fighting, you remember your parents and how the house felt. But...you said too much just now, Ami-chan. Please just apologize and let it end here."

There was a bit of a pause.

"Sorry, Minori-chan. I said way too much. Could you forget it all?"

Ami lowered her head slightly. Seeing that, Minori slowly and loudly clapped her hands together once.

"There! It's a deal. Okay, I've forgotten it!"

Finally, the air in the room relaxed.

"Actually, where is Tiger? How about we look for her for a bit?" Maya said in a much brighter voice. Everyone, probably wanting to change the mood, nodded to each other and left the room.

The sliding door of the closet *fwooshed* open.

"I feel like we saw something we really weren't meant to see!"

The first one to fall out was Kitamura. Noto and Haruta also rolled out after him.

"Actually, Miss Kushieda is kinda...like how do I put this...I'm really, really glad that I didn't ask her anything weird, now."

"Am I the only one who didn't get the point of their fight at all? How is Ami-chan involved in this? Taka-chan, what's going on?"

"That's what I want to know! Really! Everyone...everyone is just..." Disoriented, Ryuuji crawled from the closet.

"You...you...you baaaaaastaaaaaaaaards..."

Her wet hair disheveled, her face red from wrath—among other things—Taiga was breathing heavily as she got up. It stood to reason. He had done all of those things to the Palmtop Tiger. He had asked for this.

Ryuuji closed his eyes and waited in silence. He prepared himself for a slap with the weight of her whole body in it, but Taiga's right hand just passed limply through the air. She drifted to the ground, sat with her legs folded to the side, and pitifully hid her red face in her hands.

"This is just too awkward! What is this... Why did you have to involve me in something like this?! It doesn't hurt you—you can just go back to your rooms and be fine! I have to pretend that

I don't know anything for two more nights and pretend to be upbeat when Minorin and Dimhuahua are so on edge! I need to put on an act..."

"Oh, right, that's pretty hard."

"Shuddup, you brainless, hairy caterpillar! But, but, really what is this... Why are Minorin and Dimhuahua fighting? Maybe I shouldn't have told Dimhuahua everything..."

There wasn't a single person who could answer Taiga's question. The boys could only look at each other uneasily, still overwhelmed by the fight that they shouldn't have seen.

"Anyway..." Kitamura said in a low voice, his glasses still half-way down his face. "We didn't see anything. Aisaka met Takasu on the way back to her room and was talking to him in the hall-way. When she came back, it seemed the girls had been there but had gone somewhere again. That's right...right?"

Taiga somehow nodded, though her face was still hot.

"We really did something stupid, getting carried along like that." Kitamura lightly smacked his own head. Ryuuji didn't know what he meant by that, but the words didn't seem to be meant for him.

The closet perverts had successfully made their escape. Left alone by herself in the girls' room, Taiga, who had to pretend not to know anything for two days, watched them leave with an endlessly resentful gaze. "Actually, what *did* you guys come here for...?"

THE FAIR WEATHER from the day before had transformed, and that morning's sky was covered with heavy snow clouds. The weather forecast predicted a storm before noon. There was no wind at the moment, but light snow was already falling on the ski slopes.

"How are your hands, Takasu-kun?"

Turning around at Kitamura's voice, Ryuuji waved his glove-covered right hand.

"All good. Just stinging a little."

During breakfast, he had gotten a light burn—or more like, been burned by Taiga, that unrivaled klutz. In the dining hall, Taiga had been getting a second helping of miso soup when he asked her in a low voice, "So how'd it turn out?" The girls were intent on ignoring the guys that day, too, and he was trying to be inconspicuous.

Taiga's answer was, "Whaaa?!" Then she spilled her miso soup, which she'd greedily filled to the brim, on Ryuuji's hand.

"I've realized something... Never get close to Taiga while she's holding something dangerous."

"It was an accident, wasn't it? Why don't you forgive her?"

"I can't believe you're saying the same thing as Taiga... 'It wasn't on purpose! It was an accident! Oh no!' She didn't even apologize."

"There was all that stuff that happened yesterday. A lot's going on."

Just let it go. Kitamura's mouth twisted, and he raised his palms up in the air. Ryuuji just raised his eyebrows slightly in response.

The morning was their free time.

He could see people laughing as they started to practice skiing and began falling over. There were even some people in the process of making snowmen. Noto and Haruta were probably long gone up the lift, headed to the courses.

"You don't have to hang around with me. You can go to the courses."

"I was planning on teaching you how to turn today, Takasu."

"It's fine. I'm okay."

Kitamura wouldn't be able to enjoy skiing with Ryuuji around, and knowing how intense Kitamura could get about teaching, he wanted to be spared the lesson.

"No matter what I do, I can't get a feel for it. Taiga's staying back, too. She's probably pulling her sled over there, anyway, so I'll join her."

They waved at each other as Kitamura went off towards the lift, and they parted ways. Ryuuji walked towards the gently inclining edge of the slopes.

Whether Taiga had stayed behind or not, there was something he wanted to think about on his own. His head was so muddled that there was no way he could have fun skiing with his friends.

The snow sucked at his boots as he walked. It was a lot colder than the day before, and his face stung. He slowly advanced towards the lodge that acted as a rest area at the bottom of the slopes, doing his best not to fall.

Asking about Minori's true feelings, or even knowing what her true intentions were, didn't amount to anything. He felt like his heart had been knocked right out of him, like a disastrous game of Jenga, and other pieces of himself were collapsing into the spot where it had been. He was helpless, in pain, and it didn't seem relief was coming anytime soon.

Ryuuji inhaled and rubbed his eyes. He hadn't slept much the day before. He knew that thinking about it wouldn't do anything and that Minori's feelings wouldn't change no matter how much he thought about it, but the fight he'd witnessed had kept going around and around in his mind all night.

He had a vague feeling that there was something that Ami and Minori had both agreed on not saying out loud in that fight. There was something that Ryuuji didn't know about, and it was eating away at him.

If that were the case, then there was something that even Ami was hiding from him.

He breathed out white as he thought about it. There was something that Minori, Ami, Taiga and Kitamura all couldn't talk about, but at the same time, desperately wanted to say. If they'd just come out with it, the gears might turn without disharmony or deception.

But no one said it. They couldn't say it. They were scared that exposing everything might bring them to a point of no return. They were nervous, and so they swallowed their words. *They'll get it even if I don't say anything, right? They'll understand, right? We'll understand each other, right?*

But of course, they still wanted to talk about it. And sometimes it would show itself like a needle, poking at them.

He looked around at the gaudy gear of the people scattered across the slopes and found Taiga. She was with Minori. They were riding a sled together, laughing. He didn't have any reason to intrude on them when they were like that, so Ryuuji turned around.

His eyes came upon Ami.

"Oh," he said. "What are you doing in a place like this?"

"My ankle hurts a little bit, so I'm resting."

Squatting down in the soft snow few people made their way to, Ami was gloomily building a snow mountain by herself. He was taken aback by her reply—she had been crabby and spiteful, telling him that she hated him because he was stupid for so long, after all.

Plus, there was all the stuff that happened the day before. Ryuuji was a little uneasy as he walked towards her.

"Did you fall down...?"

Ami had stuck her rental skis and poles up in the snow behind her. "Yeah. I'm tired, and I can't even go to get coffee at the lodge because I forgot my wallet."

"So now you're making a mountain by yourself?"

"It's not a mountain. This is supposed to be Kamakura—like the city in the mountains."

If that's supposed to be Kamakura, it's sort of doomed. Even Ryuuji, an absolute amateur when it came to snow, couldn't help but think that as he watched Ami's gloved hands pat the small, fragile mound.

"Aren't you supposed to start out by rolling a snowball like you're making a snowman instead of making a giant pile of snow?"

"I'm fine with this."

Ami stayed stubbornly crouched down and continued to build the mountain. She placed the snow she scooped up with her gloved hand on the mound and patted it down. No matter how long she did that, it wouldn't end up becoming the Kamakura she wanted.

I understand, even if you don't say anything, Ryuuji thought as he watched her face, which seemed to be reflecting the white snow. The previous day's dispute with Minori had gotten to Ami in the end. That was why she was alone here, meaninglessly gathering snow to pass the time. It was like she was churning through her own messed-up mind.

"Oh, hey!"

"I'm just helping you."

He sat across from her and started to pile up more snow. He didn't intend to try to comfort her, or get more information about the fight, or anything of that sort. He hadn't forgotten that she'd said she hated him because he was stupid, either.

It was just that Ryuuji was also alone. No matter how much time passed, it wasn't as though Ami's Kamakura would be done. It wasn't as though he felt like he could leave her alone there as she vainly packed together the snow. Plus, if Ami really thought he was in the way, she would have told him so.

"Hey, you have to make sure you compact it..."

"..."

"C'mon, do it. You put so much effort into piling it up when it's just gonna keep collapsing."

Ami's hands stopped, causing an avalanche above the snow Ryuuji had piled up. It started to collapse, and resigned, Ryuuji stretched out his hand to pat it down.

"Oh?!"

Ami stuck her head face first into the mountain. She did it with the energy of the drunkest person at a party sticking their face into a cake as a joke.

"What the heck are you doing?! Isn't it cold?! Is this some kind of beauty treatment?!" Ryuuji exclaimed. She stayed like that for a few seconds. "Excuse me, but—"

Finally, Ami lifted her head. Snow stuck to her eyelashes and eyebrows. Her cheeks and nose had flushed bright red from the cold.

"There's something I need to tell you, Takasu-kun..."

"Hey, I get it, I get it. There's probably a lot you've got to say. For starters, how about you apologize for calling me an idiot?"

"That's not what I meant. It's not...that."

Ami rested her chin on the peak of the collapsed snow pile and quietly closed her eyes. She took a breath through her nose, held it for a while, and then took another.

"It might be my fault that Minori-chan rejected you..." she said.

Ryuuji just looked at Ami's face. *Wha?* he mouthed without a sound.

"Earlier...when you weren't around, I said something nasty to Minori-chan. I don't even know why I said it, but I can't take it back. I think Minori-chan's been thinking about it for a long time, and that's why she rejected you."

He couldn't understand what she meant. "Uhhh...well any-way...what was it that you said?"

"Are you angry? Ha ha. I guess anyone would be angry."

"Well, it's not like I can say anything about it if I don't know the details."

"I can't tell you."

There it was. Another thing no one could talk about.

"Plus, yesterday, I started a fight with Minori. I said some nasty things I regret, but I still get annoyed whenever I look at her face. I can't help it. There are a lot of things that annoy me, but the main thing is that she absolutely won't talk straight to anyone. No matter how much I tried to start a fight, I couldn't get Minori-chan to actually say what she was feeling."

Her long eyelashes cast down, Ami slowly extended her hand.

She smashed the mountain of snow violently. She chopped at it until it was utterly destroyed. Then she took a breath.

"I don't like you because you're an idiot..."

"That again..."

"I hate myself because I'm an idiot, too. I—"

As though she'd exhausted herself, she sat down in the middle of the mess of snow she had made. She brushed away the ruins of the snow mountain with her hands, breaking it down, scattering it around, and then looked up at the dull, silver sky.

"Hey, Takasu-kun."

It was starting to snow harder, and the slivers of ice adhered to Ami's hair. Ryuuji could only look at her, hung up on finding the words he should have said.

"Apparently Taiga's been trying to become independent recently. Minori-chan just straight out rejected you. They've both let go of your hands now, and I was thinking that maybe, I'd grab your hand instead. Actually, this all went exactly to plan. I've always been thinking of trying to ask you out. Because I like you. What would you do if I said that? None of it is true, though."

She said it all faster than he could understand.

"You said that way too fast! You didn't even give me a chance to be surprised before you turned everything around!"

Trying to gain control over his leaping heart, Ryuuji desperately rubbed at his own face. His snow-covered gloves made his already freezing nose grow even colder.

Ami didn't even smile as she simply stared at Ryuuji.

"But none of it's true, anyway. If you believed that, it wouldn't be according to plan. I didn't want it to end up this way. But, well...I really did stick my nose into something I shouldn't have."

Her mouth touched the snow. It melted as it was touched. The faint smile that finally came over her lips vanished just as quickly.

"I'm racked with guilt... I'm self-destructing, too. This is what happened because of all my mistakes."

"This is what happened... By that, do you mean Kushieda rejecting me? I don't want you to take the blame for that. I don't know what happened between you and Kushieda, but I'm not the kind of person who blames other people for being rejected."

"Right..."

Ami sniffled and got up slowly. Then, with her usual cute and perfect smile, she looked down at Ryuuji.

"Well then, shall we end this friendship?"

"Huh?"

Ami took her gloves off, put them under her arm, and made rings with her thumbs and pointer fingers. "Break it off, break our ties," she said in a sing-song voice, and then pulled the rings apart.

"Why are you breaking it off with me..."

"Because you're an idiot and I hate you...so, it's punishment."

That made two people who hated each other for being idiots, now. Without saying who exactly was being punished, or for what, Ami turned around.

What is this?

Words just weren't enough.

Ryuuji watched her go, frozen and at a loss for words.

"DIMHUAHUA, GET OUTTA THE WAAAAAAAAA-AAAAAAAAY!"

"I'M NOT DOING IT ON PURPOSE! I'M NOT DOING IT ON PURPOSE! I'M NOT DOING IT ON PURPOSEEEEEEEE!'"

Taiga and Minori shot into view, roaring over on a sled. Though they had their feet desperately outstretched, they were going too fast to stop. Dumbfounded, Ryuuji could only watch as, first, Taiga tumbled off the sled, scattering the snow. Next, losing her balance, Minori was also thrown off.

The unmanned sled knocked over Ami and continued sliding back to the entrance to the slopes.

"I told you to get out of the way..." Taiga scowled as she dug Ami out of the snow.

"Y...youuu! Just how many times do you need to fall off that sled before you're done?! Are you an idiot?! Why'd you keep riding that sled?! Just walk around on the snow, you numbskull!"

"That's why I'm a-pol-o-giz-ing. I know! I'll get you a soft-serve ice cream at the lodge. My treat."

"I don't neeeeeed that! It's freezing, you idiot!"

Ami's angry kicks connected with Taiga's butt, but the oversized gear protected her, and it didn't seem to have much of an effect.

"Soooorry, Ahmin! S-sorry we couldn't stop... Forgive us! I'm sorry!" Minori rushed over to apologize, too.

"Why would I forgive you?!" Ami glared at Minori as her voice cracked. "It was on purpose, wasn't it?! That had to be on purpose! I felt murder coming off of you!"

"What?! No, no, of course not. We just couldn't stop, is all!"

"That was so on purpose! I'm just going to say it—you're still angry about what happened yesterday, right?! You came to interfere, didn't you?! That's definitely what this is! I know it!"

Ami's cheeks and eyes turned bright red as she shouted. There was a blood vessel popping on her temple that looked so cartoonish it might burst. Her nose was red, too, and then to top it all off, she threw snow at Minori.

She scored a lucky hit right in Minori's face. Minori staggered for a moment.

"Whaaaaat?! Are you talking about how you were trying to start a fight with me, Ahmin?! I let that go, but you're the one who's bringing it back up again!"

Ahhh... Taiga and Ryuuji's eyes met. *You stop them—No, you stop them,* they communicated silently.

However, the two of them weren't supposed to know anything about what happened in the girls' room last night. Intervening would be difficult.

"What do you mean you let it go?! You've been ignoring me ever since this morning!"

"That's because there was nothing to talk about! Or is it that I've got to entertain you or else I'm ignoring you?!"

"The way you look down on me has really been bugging me! You brawn-for-brains woman!"

"Who's looking down on you?! Maybe you're just getting carried away because I'm trying to be the better person?!"

Bam! Minori's hands came down on Ami's shoulders.

"Why you..."

Ami seemed like she was going to return the favor, but Minori quickly grabbed hold of Ami's hand and gave her a solid smack. They glared at each other. When it came to reflexes, Ami was no match for Minori.

"Don't you dare hit my face!"

"It's not like you're an actress!"

Their voices echoed across the snow-covered mountain as they stomped their feet. Ami's voice was like a high-pitched shriek.

"I-I've always hated you, just so you know! You've always annoyed the hell out of me!"

"Oh, I see! And who cares about that? I don't care whether you hate me or not—it doesn't hurt or bug me at all!" Minori wasn't backing down. Their argument got even more heated.

"I hate you! I hate you! I hate you! I hate everything about you!!!"

"Same here! I don't care about you at all! I'll never listen to you again!"

"Oh, I'd love that!"

"Actually, why haven't you just gone back to your old school?! Hurry up and go back where you belong!"

"That has nothing to do with youuuu?! You pauper! Go work at part-time jobs your whole life!"

"What'd you say?! Why don't you put some makeup on that fake face and go back to modeling your whole life?!"

"Whaaaat?!"

They had crossed the line into saying things that should have remained unspoken. Their quarrel was accelerating. They jabbed intermittently at each other's shoulders, getting to the point they were doing it harder than they would have if they were joking.

"You want to do this?!"

"I won't apologize even if you start crying!"

"I have to go back up Minorin! Let's go, Ryuuji! Why you, Dimhuahua!"

"Hey! You got it wrong, dummy! Stop that!"

"This is such a terrifying scene! It's like a nightmare!"

"Your fight with the patriarch was way scarier! Your nose was bleeding all over!"

People around them had noticed the shouting and were beginning to gather around in curiosity. Just then, Taiga and Ryuuji pulled them apart.

"Ah!"

Only Taiga saw it.

The orange hairpin holding up Minori's bangs flew off as Ami's hand hit it. It fell a little ways away on top of the fresh snow. Ami and Minori's quarrel was still violent, and no one else had noticed the hairpin.

Trying to not lose sight of it, Taiga ran towards the pin. It was precious. She absolutely could not let it get lost. Her legs sank into the soft snow, and she reached out her hand.

"...Uh."

Suddenly, there was nothing under her sunken foot. She didn't even have time to scream as the snow in front of her eyes gave way, and she fell.

Maya, Nanako, and Kitamura came running up.

"Get a hold of yourselves! What are you two doing?!"

"But—but—but—she! It's not my fault!"

"All I did was respond to her trying to start a fight!"

When they finally pulled the two apart, even the bachelorette (age 30) had come over. Ami was held back by Kitamura, seething as she breathed hard. Minori was glaring at Ami while grinding her teeth. A group had gathered, murmuring in surprise at the unusual confrontation between Minori and Ami. The two were surrounded.

Even Ryuuji was surprised. How had it gotten this bad?

"Anyway, you go with Kushieda and have her calm down—Taiga?"

Huh? He looked around. He realized he couldn't find Taiga, even though he thought she had been beside him.

"Taiga's not here..."

Minori turned around as she heard him mutter. She stopped glaring at Ami. Her eyes went wide as she looked up at Ryuuji.

"She was here just a second ago. She was with you, trying to stop the fight..."

"Taiga..."

Minori looked around, taking in her surroundings. Then her gaze stopped. At around the same time, Ryuuji saw it, too.

It was the footprints of a single person in the snow. Minori shook herself free from Ryuuji's grasp on her shoulders. She walked to follow those footprints, and Ryuuji continued after her.

"These...huh, it—it couldn't be. Taiga..."

"N-no way..."

They realized that the snow piled up a bit and then dropped off into a cliff. They also noticed formations of jutting snow that had fallen down. When they looked down, they held their breaths as a strong gust of wind assaulted them.

On the steep slope where the Japanese cedars grew, they found the traces of someone who had fallen. They didn't know how far the tracks went.

Apparently the Palmtop Tiger's missing.

Was the kid who disappeared from Class C the Palmtop Tiger?!

Gathered in the large hall of the lodge, the second years were causing a commotion. Beyond the fogged-up windows, the weather outside was stormy, as predicted by the forecast. The snow was striking down. It was a blizzard.

"Takasu-kun, I just heard back from Ms. Koigakubo about what's going on. Apparently, the slope Aisaka fell down is a conifer forest, and the road under it is closed during the winter. The people in charge of the ski resort are searching from the road, but if they can't find her, they're going to leave it to the police... Takasu!"

"Ugh..."

Kitamura clapped in front of Ryuuji's face, making him finally raise his head in surprise at the sound.

"Get a hold of yourself! They'll definitely find her, so it'll be okay!"

"Uh...right."

That was all he could muster. He was sitting on a hard chair carved from a log. Ryuuji felt like he was in a bad dream. He dropped his eyes to the faint, red burn on his right hand. *That klutz*, he groaned in the back of his throat.

At long last, that klutz—Taiga—had gone and made a fatal blunder.

He had even seen her fall down a flight of stairs right before his eyes. She fell down, crashed into things, spilled stuff, got knocked down—those kinds of things were everyday occurrences for her. Just the other day, she was almost run over by a car. His burned right hand was proof of Taiga's blunders.

And yet despite that, Taiga had never really injured herself until now. Her miraculous luck had held up so far, but at long last, it had come to this.

He blamed himself for not immediately noticing she'd disappeared from his side, and those feelings were swirling inside his head. She'd just disappeared—just like the night of the Christmas Eve party. He prayed that it was the same this time.

Back then, Taiga had been safe at home. Once he noticed she was missing, he ran back to her.

But this time...

Even looking out the window was too terrifying. He imagined what would happen if they didn't find her in this weather and then immediately drowned it out. That couldn't happen. That would absolutely not happen. Taiga was a klutz, but on the other hand, she had good reflexes, and her body was strangely sturdy. She would come up with something. It would absolutely work out. It would.

Bringing his hands together as if in prayer, Ryuuji squeezed his eyes shut. He didn't notice the worried looks coming from Noto and Haruta across from him.

In a corner of his mind, he still couldn't help but think the unavoidable. If only he could rewind time—if only he could go back to that moment—he absolutely would not have taken his eyes off Taiga. He would have grabbed Taiga's hand and never let go.

Even if people suspected they had a father-daughter-like relationship, even if it got in the way of Taiga living alone, even if it got in the way of their love lives—he would never let go of Taiga's hand again. If anyone said anything about their relationship, he'd just ignore them.

"What a crazy blizzard..."

Ryuuji turned around.

In the seat right behind Ryuuji's, Minori was glaring out the window. She pursed her lips tightly and pulled her beanie down low. She put on her gloves and zipped her gear all the way to the top. Ryuuji had a bad feeling.

"Kushieda...what do you think you're doing?"

"Look at that blizzard. We've got to find her fast. I'm going out to look."

As soon as she stood up, he grabbed her in a panic.

"Are you an idiot?! You'll get into an accident, too!"

"I can't just stay here doing nothing! It's fine, I'll definitely come right back! Just let me go where we went before and back! I'll come back after that!"

She didn't wait for an answer but shook her arm free of Ryuuji's grip. Minori actually started walking out.

"Don't," Kitamura yelled, but Minori didn't listen. She freed herself from Kitamura's attempts to grab her as well, and kept going steadily down the wooden stairs to the first floor. No matter how many times Ryuuji grabbed her shoulder, she swatted him away, and eventually, he resolved himself.

"Damn it...then I'm going, too!"

"I'll go, too! Noto! Haruta! Tell the teacher that we left!" Kitamura yelled.

"Whaa?! You can't!" Noto and the others stood up in surprise, but Ryuuji couldn't stop Minori, and they couldn't let her go alone, either.

What are we going to do?! Noto and Haruta ran to where the teachers were. Behind them, Ami sat alone, her pale face lowered. She was silent, and her expression didn't change.

As the regular ski guests retreated from the storm, Ryuuji and Kitamura desperately followed Minori. Snow piled up along the edges of their goggles in the blink of an eye and pulled at their feet. At last, Ryuuji grabbed hold of Minori's arm, and Kitamura grabbed her from the other side.

"Don't rush, Kushieda! If we're really going to try finding Aisaka, we need to calm down and look around!"

"..."

Minori finally turned around and grimaced. Her shoulders shook as she took a harsh breath and gave him a single nod.

The blowing snowstorm seemed to be pushing them back as the three continued forward with their arms locked together. The place where Minori and Ami fought wasn't far from the lodge. It was just at the foot of the slopes.

"Around here, there were traces that she slipped!"

Minori seemed excited as she quickly got as close to the cliff as she could. She pointed at some piled snow that seemed to have concealed the marks.

"Watch out! Don't get too close!"

"But she's somewhere below this isn't she?! Taigaaaaaaa! Answer meeeeee!"

Ryuuji braced his boots desperately to keep from falling and grabbed Minori's sleeve as she stretched to look down. Right before his eyes, the snow at the tips of Minori's boots began to crumble. He felt cold sweat on his back.

As he supported Minori, he looked down at the trees growing on the snowy slope. He couldn't see the bottom. If it wasn't for the blizzard, they might have been able to see traces of where she fell down.

"What's that...?"

Something shone in the snow.

It was way ahead of where they had been looking. It was in the shadow of the slope, right below where they looked. The small, orange thing twinkled like a single shining star in a night sky the color of snow.

It really was tiny, like it might be covered by the falling and gathering snow any moment now. But Ryuuji could clearly see it.

"Taiga!"

She'd fallen while trying to pick it up. If that was the case, if they went down using that as a landmark, they were sure to find her.

"Huh?! You saw something?! Was Taiga there?! Did you find her?!"

"Probably! Hurry, call someone... No, we might lose sight of it... Dammit! Kushieda, go call a teacher, or any adult, over here! Kitamura, stay here. If I don't come back up, pull me up or call for help!"

"No, I'll—" Minori tried to say something and then held it back. "Okay!"

With one quick nod, she ran off into the blizzard. Using Kitamura as a landmark, Ryuuji slid down the slope on his butt.

It was too steep to walk down. He slipped a bit and grabbed a tree, then slipped again and clung to another. When his leg would get buried, he would pull it out. What he was headed for was the incredibly tiny light of the hairpin.

Don't disappear, no matter what, don't disappear, Ryuuji practically screamed as he desperately went down the slope. *I'm almost there*, he wheezed as he grasped at the snow. He wiped at the ice on his goggles.

He might have gone down twenty meters. It was a place not visible from the road below. He reached below the branches of the overgrown evergreens, grabbed the hairpin, and looked around.

"T-Taiga!"

He found her almost immediately nearby.

Halfway buried in the soft snow, Taiga had fallen in a space between the roots of a large tree, her body curled up into a ball. Being careful not to tumble down himself, he approached that hollow by crawling. Burying his boots deep in the snow to secure his footing, Ryuuji stretched out his arm and pulled at her small body.

"Taiga! Taiga! Taiga!"

As he brought her up from the snow, Taiga's head limply fell back. He supported her neck as he pulled her up. Her neck was warm, and she had a pulse. She had probably hit her head on a tree as she fell down. He saw something red on her forehead and held his breath.

For the first time in his life, he felt a trembling sensation start from the bottom of his stomach and make its way up his spine.

"Ow..."

He heard a small voice. Taiga's eyelashes trembled, and she grimaced. She was alive. She was safe.

Ryuuji took in a deep breath, exhaled, and stared up the slope. He didn't have time to think or even to feel relieved. He held Taiga's 40 kilograms to him as he began to crawl up the snowy slope on all fours. Whenever he took a step, the snow collapsed and turned into a small avalanche that went down the cliff. He couldn't brace himself.

They might have no choice but to wait there for help. He groaned, feeling absolutely powerless, but then in that moment Taiga's arm moved. She was clinging to Ryuuji's torso.

"I fell... It hurts..." she groaned deliriously. If Taiga could hold on to him, that changed the situation.

He buried himself up to the knees in snow again. Grasping the branches and roots of the trees protruding from the snow,

Ryuuji continued to crawl back up the slope. He wanted to talk to Taiga, but this wasn't the time. He ground his teeth. He had to focus everything on moving forward without dropping her.

"Ryuuji..."

Taiga's hand touched his face. *Clack*. Her gloveless hand felt the goggles. She might have mistaken them for glasses.

"Oh...Kitamura-kun?"

Taiga was mistaken.

He didn't mind. Or rather, this wasn't the time for him to correct her. He just needed to keep crawling up.

"I thought you were Ryuuji... In times like these, the one who comes to save me...is always Ryuuji... Sorry... I'm sorry..."

The voice he heard was strangely bright. But there was something unfocused about it, like she was talking in her sleep. Taiga wasn't completely conscious. Her voice was fluttery, high-pitched, and more absent than usual.

She continued to whisper into Ryuuji's ear.

"Kitamura-kun, you know...you didn't really help much..."

His foot slipped wildly. Ryuuji screamed in the back of his throat. If Taiga hadn't been holding on to him, he would have lost his balance, and they would have both fallen.

"Sorry, but you're not really doing that great as the Patron Saint of Broken Hearts... The thing I asked for didn't come true at all... My feelings for Ryuuji just won't go away... I wanted to become stronger...but it didn't work..."

Ryuuji grabbed Taiga's clothes as she began to slip. He ground his teeth even harder, held her as firmly as he could, and looked up.

He could see Kitamura. Kitamura was looking at him and yelling something. It was just a bit further.

"I just like Ryuuji, no matter what I do... I want things to work out for him with Minorin... It's so hard. It's just so hard, everything is so hard... I can't..."

"..."

"I'm no good, right...? I wanted to do my best, being alone... I kept saying that I'd get through it, but it was all talk... In the end...all I could do was wait to be saved... I'm weak, weak...weak... I hate it..."

Tears fell from Taiga's still closed eyes. Then her hands relaxed. Suddenly the weight of her whole body was on his arm. Ryuuji desperately directed all his strength into his right arm. He pulled Taiga's torso with all of his strength, but his foot slipped, and he lost his balance.

They would fall—they were falling—

"Huh?!"

There was a sturdy hand being offered right before his eyes. Adults wearing matching gaudy fluorescent outfits came down one after another, and in the blink of an eye, lightly lifted Ryuuji and Taiga along with them. It was the people from the ski resort, or maybe the police.

"Are you okay?! You're not hurt?!"

"I'm not! But Taiga! There's blood, here..."

He didn't care what they were or who they were. Ryuuji wailed desperately at someone who handed him a blanket. *We got it*, the adults in the fluorescent clothes answered with nods and ran off carrying Taiga.

He couldn't even sit. He just fell onto the snow and gasped. His vision was painted over white—it was the blizzard. The blizzard has penetrated all the way into his head.

He realized that Minori had rushed over to his side. Kitamura, too. Finally, he knew what it was that they couldn't tell him. He also knew how stupid he had been.

The knot that held everything together had been undone. It had been pulled too hard, and the string was tearing.

"Kitamura... I need a favor."

Ryuuji rested his head on the borrowed shoulder of his worried friend. "Could you say that you were the one who went down to save Taiga just now? If Taiga asks, tell her you didn't hear anything. Taiga was unconscious the entire time. She didn't say anything. Please tell her that...please!"

Kitamura supported Ryuuji's jacket-clad back. "I didn't say anything because Aisaka asked me to keep it a secret, but—"

Through the goggles, he couldn't see Kitamura's expression.

"During the new year, I happened to run into Aisaka. She seemed really depressed and seriously asked me...if she could pay respects to me as the Patron Saint of Broken Hearts. Does it have anything to do with that?"

Ryuuji didn't answer. He couldn't answer. If he opened his mouth, he didn't know what kind of sound he would make.

"So it does... Right. So, that happened on Christmas Eve, and then New Year's happened. I see..."

No one was at fault. It's not your fault. Kitamura's words were blown away in the blizzard.

In the end, Taiga was mostly uninjured. God had definitely given her a sturdy body suitable for a klutz.

When they sat down for dinner, the teachers recounted that she just had a small graze on her temple. Apparently, she just wanted to die from embarrassment at causing such a fuss.

Ryuuji heard relieved voices from all over the place, but some tactless individual raised their hand and asked, "Does that mean we can see her tomorrow?"

However, the bachelorette's (age 30) response was surprising.

"Well, Aisaka-san will spend the night in the hospital, and then tomorrow, her mother will pick her up. So, she's going home ahead of us. It'd be hard for her to travel by bus again like that."

Without thinking, Ryuuji dropped his chopsticks.

Her mother—did that mean her real mother? Was her mother, who didn't even come when Taiga was suspended, who had never so much as shown up at their school, going to come to this remote ski resort? Even when Taiga was practically uninjured?

"That's great, isn't it, Taka-kun?! Tiger's gonna be fine~!"

"Uh, yeah…"

Haruta's eyes stopped on Ryuuji's chest pocket. "Huh? So that hairpin ended up getting back to you, huh, Taka-chan?"

Ryuuji had stuck it unthinkingly in his pocket when he picked it up from the snow. Haruta whispered in his ear like an idiot, "Actually, is this the Christmas present that you tried to give…that person before? You threw away wrapping paper with trees on it, too, didn't you? I saw it, but I didn't understand what it meant until now…"

"Basically…"

Ryuuji's head was still in the middle of a storm. Even as he shrugged his shoulders in affirmation, he wasn't seeing anything around him at all. There was too much to think about.

That was why he hadn't noticed. Sitting just a bit away from them, a certain person had turned herself into a full-body radar unit as she tried to eavesdrop on what Ryuuji had to say. When she heard their conversation, she immediately understood.

She understood the results of everything she had been doing on purpose and even the things she'd done completely unintentionally.

Without anyone seeing, she stood up silently and ran from the noisy, boisterous dining room. She jogged out into the freezing hallway and arrived at the unoccupied lounge.

She collapsed onto the sofa that Ryuuji had been sitting on the night before.

She clutched her knees and buried her face as tears ran under her hands. She didn't know why she was sad, but she knew only that she hated her thin, girlish hands. She absolutely hated her hands, which were only good for hiding her face as she cried.

Alone, Minori covered her face with her hands, shrinking smaller and smaller into a ball as she cried soundlessly for some time.

The blizzard was supposed to end the next day.

However, the sound of the wind throwing snow against the windows was fierce. It blew violently enough to freeze their feet, even as it continued to shake the windows.

Afterword

SO...I HAVE A DOCUMENT where I keep track of important things like my internet IDs and passwords. (I put it in an envelope that says something like, "Important, so keep it safe!") I made it nearly ten years ago and thought, "This is so important, I'm sure I'll lose it." And...I lost it! One day, the envelope that had survived moving twice suddenly vanished from the spot it should have been in.

I looked for it everywhere but couldn't find it. I looked for it in my work desk drawers, the closet, the shelves, the dresser, the kitchen, the streets at dawn...in Sakuragicho...even though there's no way it'd be there...

Wh-what'll I do now? This is just how I've been living my life lately. It's been nearly thirty years since I was born. I've lost flexibility in both my mind and body, so when I have these kinds of sudden accidents, I don't have the smarts to cope. I have no room for accommodation, I can't listen to anything, and I'll never get any taller. I'll never grow up. I can't get back what's been taken from me, either. In other words, I have only one direction left to go in—ruin!

So, I've had a ton of things taken from me. But I've also finally gotten to the eighth volume of *Toradora!* Everyone who has stayed with me so far, thank you so much! I hope you enjoyed it.

Thanks to everyone's help, I've accumulated several volumes of this series. We've gotten a manga version from Zekkyo-sensei, an anime, and...ahh! I want to tell you everything, but there's something I can't say yet! There are actually a ton of things going forward!

That's right—there've been a lot of new developments that I want you to enjoy. I haven't actually fallen into ruin. I haven't been stung by a prickly caterpillar. I don't suddenly have a ton of bumps on my right arm. "Are they hives? Is it from stress? Is it just mental?" I said as I went to the dermatologist. When I showed it to the doctor, they didn't make an instant diagnosis of, "Oh, it's caterpillar dermatitis! This is the eleventh case today! That's from the Japanese browntail moth!" I didn't go home, look up what the browntail moth looks like when it's a caterpillar, and faint for a moment, either (don't do this). It's also not super itchy, and I definitely didn't faint again on thinking that if I scratched it, the stingers from the caterpillars would prick me from inside my skin. (If only I didn't know what they looked like...)

So, everyone! I'm really grateful that you read *Toradora!* Volume 8 right up to the very end. I plan to keep working quickly on *Toradora!* Volume 9. I hope that you enjoy it! Yasu-sensei and Manager-sama, I feel like the next volume will be an ordeal as well, so please don't fall to ruin as we work hard together!

—Yuyuko Takemiya

ARTIST'S AFTERWORD

I'm so indebted to Yuyuko-sensei!

Thanks so much for your hard work!

Yay! It's tarako roe, yay!

I'm Zekkyo, and I'm in charge of making *Toradora!* into a manga series!

Everyone in *Toradora!* is so cute that I'm all smiles.

Will this really be in the volume? Will it really be printed in the volume?

Ha ha! Are you playing a trick on me?

Actually...so this is just between us, but when they let me meet Yuyuko-sensei the other day, we actually talked about tarako. I was like, "Wow, she really is serious."

Toradora! is so much fun! I'm rooting for it to do well.

—ZEKKYO

Experience these great light novel titles from Seven Seas Entertainment